Cash's heart  **breath gone, a** **he stared at** **the doorway.**

"Jasmine." Her name was out before he could call it back.

She looked startled, as if she hadn't seen him standing at the back of the office.

His heart lodged in his throat, his senses telling him something his mind refused to accept now that her car had been found. Jasmine was *alive?*

"I...I..." She started to turn as if to leave and he finally found his feet, lunging forward to stop her, half afraid she was nothing more than a puff of smoke that would vanish the moment he touched her.

She took a step back, seeming afraid, definitely startled. Cash stopped just feet from her, struggling to believe what was before his eyes. My God, could it really be her? Jasmine?

Alive?

Dear Harlequin Intrigue Reader,

You won't be able to resist a single one of our May books. We have a lineup so shiver inducing that you may forget summer's almost here!

- *Executive Bodyguard* is the second book in Debra Webb's exciting new trilogy, THE ENFORCERS. For the thrilling conclusion, be sure you pick up *Man of Her Dreams* in June.

- Amanda Stevens concludes her MATCHMAKERS UNDERGROUND series with *Matters of Seduction*. And the Montana McCalls are back, in B.J. Daniels's *Ambushed!*

- We also have two special premiers for you. Kathleen Long debuts in Harlequin Intrigue with *Silent Warning*, a chilling thriller. And LIPSTICK LTD., our special promotion featuring sexy, sassy sleuths, kicks off with Darlene Scalera's *Straight Silver*.

- A few of your favorite Harlequin Intrigue authors have some special books you'll love. Rita Herron's *A Breath Away* is available this month from HQN Books. And, in June, Joanna Wayne's *The Gentlemen's Club* is being published by Signature Spotlight.

Harlequin Intrigue brings you the best in breathtaking romantic suspense with six fabulous books to enjoy. Please write to us—we love to hear from our readers.

Sincerely,

Denise O'Sullivan
Senior Editor
Harlequin Intrigue

AMBUSHED!
B.J. DANIELS

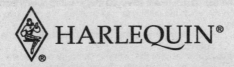

HARLEQUIN®

TORONTO • NEW YORK • LONDON
AMSTERDAM • PARIS • SYDNEY • HAMBURG
STOCKHOLM • ATHENS • TOKYO • MILAN • MADRID
PRAGUE • WARSAW • BUDAPEST • AUCKLAND

This book is dedicated to Teagan and Hayden.
Thank you, baby girls, for all the hugs and kisses.
I can't tell you what the tea parties with you two
mean to me. I love you both dearly.

ISBN 0-373-22845-7

AMBUSHED!

Copyright © 2005 by Barbara Heinlein

This edition published by arrangement with Harlequin Books S.A.

® and TM are trademarks of the publisher. Trademarks indicated with
® are registered in the United States Patent and Trademark Office, the
Canadian Trade Marks Office and in other countries.

www.eHarlequin.com

Printed in U.S.A.

ABOUT THE AUTHOR

A former award-winning journalist, B.J. had thirty-six short stories published before her first romantic suspense, *Odd Man Out,* came out in 1995. Her book *Premeditated Marriage* won *Romantic Times* Best Intrigue award for 2002 and she received a Career Achievement Award for Romantic Suspense. B.J. lives in Montana with her husband, Parker, three springer spaniels, Zoey, Scout and Spot, and a temperamental tomcat named Jeff. She is a member of Kiss of Death, the Bozeman Writer's Group and Romance Writers of America. When she isn't writing, she snowboards in the winters and camps, water-skis and plays tennis in the summers. To contact her, write: P.O. Box 183, Bozeman, MT 59771 or look for her online at www.bjdaniels.com.

Books by B.J. Daniels

CAST OF CHARACTERS

Molly Kilpatrick—Desperate for a place to hide, she made the mistake of stealing the wrong woman's identity.

Sheriff Cash McCall—For seven years he prayed that his fiancée was alive—but not for the reason anyone suspected. Now he's falling for her double—a woman marked for murder.

Jasmine Wolfe—Only her killer knows what happened to her after she disappeared seven years ago.

Teresa Clark—A bartender who never forgets a face would get herself killed.

Kerrington Landow—He is obsessed with Jasmine. But to the point where he would have done anything to have her—or make sure no one else did?

Patty Franklin—She was good at keeping other people's secrets. But does she have a few of her own she'd kept under wraps?

Bernard Wolfe—With his stepsister dead, he gets the family fortune. With her alive, he could lose everything.

Sandra Perkins Landow—She and Jasmine shared more than a room. They shared a man and that could be deadly.

Vince Winslow—After fifteen years in prison, he only wants to find Molly and get what he has coming.

Angel Edwards—Prison made him more bloodthirsty. Pity anyone who gets in his way.

Chapter One

The abandoned barn loomed out of the rain soaked land-scape, the roof partially gone, a gaping black hole where the doors had once been.

Sheriff Cash McCall pulled his patrol car up next to Humphrey's pickup. Through the blurred thumping of the wipers, Cash could see Humphrey Perkins behind the steering wheel, waiting.

Cash cut the engine and listened to the steady drum of the rain on the patrol car roof, not anxious to go inside that barn. Hadn't he known? Hadn't he always known?

Steeling himself, he pulled up the hood on his rain-coat and stepped out of the patrol car. Humphrey didn't move, just watched as Cash walked past his pickup to-ward the barn.

Five minutes ago, Humphrey had called him. "I found something, Cash." The old farmer had sounded scared, as if wishing someone else was making this call, that someone else had found what had been hidden in the barn. "You know the old Trayton homestead on the north side of the lake?"

Everyone knew the place. The land had been tied up in a family estate for years, the dilapidated house boarded up, the barn falling down. There were No Trespassing signs posted all around the property, but Humphrey owned the land to the north and had always cut through the Trayton place to fish. Seemed that hadn't changed.

"I noticed one of the barn doors had fallen off," Humphrey had said on the phone, voice cracking. "I think you'd better come out here and take a look. It looks like there's a car in there."

Cash stepped from the rain into the cold darkness of the barn. The shape under the large faded canvas tarp was obviously a car. He could see one of the tires. It was flat.

He stood, listening to the rain falling through the hole in the roof patter on the tarp. Clearly the car had been there for a long time. Years.

Wind lifted one corner of the canvas and he saw the back bumper, the Montana State University parking sticker and part of the license plate, MT 6-431. The wind dropped the tattered edge of the tarp, but Cash had seen enough of the plate to know it was the one a statewide search hadn't turned up seven years ago.

He'd been praying it wasn't her car. Not the little red sports car she'd been anxiously waiting to be delivered.

"When I get my car, I'll take you for a ride," she'd said, flirting with him from the first time he'd met her.

How many times over the years since she'd disappeared had he heard those words echo in his head? "I'll take you for a ride."

He closed his eyes, taking in huge gulps of the rank-smelling barn air. Her car had been within five miles of Antelope Flats all these years? Right under their noses?

The search had centered around Bozeman, where she was last seen. Later, even when it had gone state-wide, there wasn't enough manpower to search every old barn or building. Especially in the remote southeastern part of the state.

He tried to breathe. She'd been almost within sight of town? So close all these years?

Cash opened his eyes, scrubbed at them with the heel of his hand, each breath a labor. He turned away and saw Humphrey's huge bulk silhouetted in the barn door, the hood of his dark raincoat pulled up, his arms dangling loose at his sides.

"It's her car, isn't it?" Humphrey said from the doorway.

Cash didn't answer, couldn't. Swallowing back the bile that rose in his throat, he walked through the pouring rain to his patrol car for his camera.

He knew he should call for forensics and the state investigators to come down from Billings. He knew he should wait, do nothing, until they arrived. But he had to know if she was inside that car.

Rain pounded the barn roof and fell through the hole overhead, splattering loudly on top of the covered car as he stepped past Humphrey to aim the camera lens at the scene inside. He took photographs of the car from every angle and the inside of the barn before putting the camera back in the patrol car.

On the way to the barn again, he pulled the pair of latex gloves from his pocket and worked them on his shaking fingers. His nostrils filled with the mildewed odor of the barn as he stepped to one side of the car, picked up the edge of the tarp and pulled.

The heavy canvas slid from the car in a whoosh that echoed through the barn and sent a flock of pigeons flapping out of the rafters, startling him.

The expensive red sports car was discolored, the windows filmed over, too dirty to see inside except for about four inches where the driver's side window had been lowered.

He stared at the car, his pulse thudding in his ears. It had been summer when she disappeared. She would have had the air conditioning on. She wouldn't have put the window down while she was driving. Not with her allergies.

The rain fell harder, drumming on the barn roof as several pigeons returned, wings fluttering overhead.

He walked around the car to the other side. The left front fender was dented and scraped, the headlight broken. He stepped closer, the cop in him determined to do this by the book. Kneeling, he took out the small plastic bag and, using his pocket knife, flaked off a piece of the blue paint that had stuck in the chrome of the headlight.

Straightening, he closed the plastic bag, put the knife and bag in his pocket and carefully tried the driver's side door.

The door groaned open and he leaned down to look inside. The key was in the ignition, her sorority symbol key chain dangling from it along with the new house key—the key to the house she'd told everyone they would be living in after they were married.

The front seat was empty. He left the door open and tried the back. The rear seat was also empty. The car would have been brand new seven years ago. Which would explain why it was so clean inside.

He started to close the door when he saw something in the crack between the two front seats. He leaned in and picked up a beer cap from the brand she always drank. He started to straighten but noticed something else had fallen in the same space. A matchbook.

Cash held the matchbook up in the dim light. It was from the Dew Drop Inn, a bar in Bozeman, where she'd been attending Montana State University. Inside, three of the matches had been used. He closed the cover and put the matchbook into an evidence bag.

Shutting the back door, he stood for a moment knowing where he had to look next, the one place he'd been dreading.

He moved to the open driver's side door and reached down beside the front seat for the lever that opened the trunk. He had to grip the top of the door for a moment, steadying himself as he saw the large dark stain on the light-colored carpet floor mat under the steering wheel.

The tarp had kept the inside of the car dry over the years, the inside fairly clean, so he knew the stain on the mat wasn't from water. He knew dried blood when he saw it. The stain was large. Too large.

As he pulled the lever, the trunk popped open with a groan. He drew the small flashlight from his coat pocket and walked toward the rear of the car, the longest walk of his life.

The bodies were always in the trunk.

Taking deep breaths, he lifted the lid and pointed the flashlight beam inside. In that instant, he died a thousand deaths before he saw that what was curled inside wasn't a body. Just a quilt rolled up between a suitcase and the spare.

Cash staggered back from the car, the temporary relief making him weak. Was it possible Jasmine had been on her way to Antelope Flats? All these years he hoped she'd run off to some foreign country to live.

Instead she'd been on her way to Antelope Flats seven years ago. But why? His heart began to pound. To see him?

Or at least that's what someone wanted him to believe. Wanted the state police to believe.

He thought of the blood on the floor mat, the car hidden just miles from his office, from the old house he'd bought that Jasmine called her engagement present.

He rubbed a hand over his face, his throat raw. Jasmine wasn't living the good life in Europe, hadn't just changed her mind about everything and run off to start a new life.

He turned and walked back out into the rain, stopping next to Humphrey's pickup. The older man was sitting in the cab. He rolled down the driver's side window as Cash approached.

"I'm going to call the state investigators," Cash said, rain echoing off the hood of his jacket. "They're going to want to talk to you."

Humphrey nodded and looked past him to the barn. "Did you find her?"

Cash shook his head and started toward his patrol car, turning to look back at the barn and the dark shadow of Jasmine's car inside. All those years of trying to forget, trying to put that part of his life behind him.

He realized now that all he'd been doing was waiting. Waiting for the other shoe to drop.

That shoe had finally dropped.

Las Vegas, Nevada

MOLLY KILPATRICK CHUCKED her clothing into her only suitcase. No time to fold anything.

Since the phone call, she'd been flying around the hotel room, grabbing up her belongings as quickly as possible. She had to skip town. It wouldn't be the first time. Or the last.

She fought back tears, trying hard not to think about Lanny. Her father's old friend was probably dead by now. He shouldn't have taken the time to warn her. He should have saved his own skin. She tried not to think about the horrible sounds she'd heard in the background before the phone went dead.

Even if the police had responded to her anonymous call immediately, they would have gotten there too late. She knew she couldn't have saved Lanny. All she could do was try to save herself.

Zipping the suitcase closed, she slid it off the bed and took one last glance around the room. She'd never owned more than she could fit into one suitcase, never stayed long in one place and made a point of never making friends. This, she knew, was why.

She'd been raised on the run, she thought, as she picked up the baseball cap from the bed and snugged it down on her short, curly blond hair.

As she passed the mirror, she checked herself, adjusting the peach-colored T-shirt over her small round breasts, tucking a pocket back into her worn jeans, glancing down at the old leather sandals before slipping on the sunglasses and picking up her purse.

She could become a chameleon when she needed to, blending into any environment. It was a talent, the one talent she'd learned from her father that she actually appreciated. Especially right now.

She didn't bother to check out since she wasn't registered anyway. For someone like her, getting past a hotel-room lock was a walk in the park.

From experience she knew that entire floors of suites were set aside for high rollers and those rooms got little use even when rented for the night. She was always gone shortly after sunrise and even the couple of times she'd been caught, she'd been able to bluff her way out of it.

She thought about picking up her last check at the café where she'd been working. It wouldn't be enough money to make it worth the risk.

Vince and Angel would find out soon enough that she'd taken off. No reason to alert them yet. It was too much to hope that the police had gotten to Lanny's quick enough to catch the two convicted felons in the act.

No, she could only assume that Vince and Angel had not only gotten away but were looking for her at this very moment. If anything, fifteen years in prison would have made them even more dangerous.

On the way through the hotel, she stopped at one of the slot machines. It was foolish. She should be getting out of there as fast as possible. But superstition was something else she'd gotten from her father. And right now she needed to test her luck to make sure it was still with her.

She dropped a quarter into the slot machine and pulled the handle. The cylinder spun, stopping on first one bar, then another and for a moment she thought she might hit the big jackpot, but the third bar blurred past.

A handful of quarters jangled into the metal tray anyway. She scooped them up. Not as lucky as she had hoped but still better than nothing, she thought as she shoved the quarters into her jeans pocket, picked up her suitcase and headed for the exit.

As she moved through the noisy casino, she looked straight ahead but noticed everything, the hectic movement of gamblers pulling one-armed bandits, change girls stopping to hand out rolls of coins, cocktail waitresses weaving through the crowds with trays of drinks.

Goodbye Vegas, she thought as she cleared the doorless opening and stepped from the air-conditioned casino into the hot desert night. She breathed in the scents, knowing she wouldn't be back here, not even sure she would be alive tomorrow. She had no idea where she would go or what she would do but it wasn't as if she hadn't done this for as long as she could remember.

As she headed toward her car parked in the huge lot, a white-haired couple came out of their RV, a homeless man cut through the cars toward the busy street and a handful of teenagers rolled through the glittering Vegas night on skateboards.

There was no one else around. But still she studied her car under the parking lot lights as she neared it. She doubted she had to worry about a car bomb. Vince and Angel preferred the personal touch. Also, they would want her alive. At least temporarily.

She unlocked the trunk of the nondescript tan sedan, put the suitcase in and slammed the lid. As she opened the driver's side door, she surreptitiously took one quick glance around and climbed in.

Not one car followed her as she wound her way through the lot and exited on a backstreet. She headed down the strip toward Interstate 15, took the first entrance ramp, and saw that she was headed north. It didn't matter where she was headed, she had no idea where she was going to go anyway.

Keeping an eye on her rearview mirror, she left the desert behind. But she knew she wasn't safe, not by any means. Vince and Angel would move heaven and earth to find her.

And they'd kill her when they did.

Chapter Two

Sheriff Cash McCall stood next to his patrol car and watched as the last of the officers came out of the old barn. They'd been searching for hours and he knew without asking that they still hadn't found her body.

He felt himself sag. He'd hoped that Jasmine's body was in the barn, that this would finally be over. He hadn't slept, couldn't get the sight of her car with the old tarp, the dented fender, the blood stain on the driver's side floor mat out of his mind.

He rubbed a hand over his face as the lead state's investigator came toward him.

John Mathews shook his head. He was a large man with a bulldog face. "We'll continue searching the farm in the morning."

Cash knew it would take days, possibly weeks, and even using the latest equipment, there was a good chance her body would never be found, that her disappearance would never be solved, that he would have to live the rest of his life without ever knowing when or if she would turn up.

"I'm sorry," Mathews said. "We didn't find anything."

Cash nodded.

Mathews had been furious when he'd realized that Cash hadn't called him immediately upon finding the car. "That was a fool thing to do. What the hell were you thinking looking in the car before we arrived?" His tone had softened. "I know how hard this must be on you. But you were her fiancée for cryin' out loud. That makes you a suspect. Especially now that her car has been found within sight of your office."

"I had to know if she was in the car," Cash said. "I took photos. I did everything by procedure."

John had sighed. "If you're smart you'll stay as far away from this investigation as physically possible."

Cash had said nothing. He knew Mathews was right but that didn't make it any easier.

Now Cash watched Mathews look past him to the lake. "We'll broaden our search to the area around the barn. When I hear something, I'll let you know."

Cash knew that was as good as it was going to get. He took off his western hat and raked a hand through his hair, unable to hide his frustration. "You know that was the year the lake was down because the new dam was being built."

"Cash," Mathews said, a clear warning in his voice. "I like you. That's why I'm going to say this to you. Stay out of it. I realize this is your turf, you know the area, your expertise might be invaluable, but don't go telling us to look in the lake, okay? If her body turns up in the lake… You know what I'm saying."

He knew exactly what Mathews was saying. He was a suspect. He'd been a suspect from the moment Jasmine disappeared seven years ago. "I just want her found."

"We all do. But you're smart enough to know that the stain under the steering wheel was blood." He nodded. "It's her blood type. Given the dent in the right front fender, the fact that the car has been hidden in the barn all these years, the amount of blood on the floor mat and the steering wheel, we're treating this as a homicide."

Cash knew that Mathews thought Jasmine had been run off the road and then attacked, possibly hitting her head on the steering wheel, or had been struck while behind the wheel by the attacker, who had then gotten rid of her body somewhere and hidden her car in the barn. Cash knew that because given the evidence as it now stood, he would have thought the same thing.

What hit home was that Jasmine really might be dead. The hidden car, the blood, seven years without anyone seeing her. There was nothing else to surmise from the evidence. The weight of it pressed down on his chest making it almost impossible to breathe. Head wounds caused significant blood loss. He couldn't keep kidding himself that she'd somehow walked away from a blow to her head.

The facts no longer gave credence to his fantasy that she'd taken off, had been living it up on some Mediterranean island all these years.

"Even if you weren't a suspect, you're too emotionally involved to work this case anyway," Mathews said.

Cash fought to curb his anger and frustration, knowing it would only strengthen Mathews' point. "Unless her disappearance is solved, I will *always* be a suspect. You have any idea what that is like?"

"You know how this works," Mathews said quietly. "You still have your job as sheriff. You think you would if anyone believed for a minute that you had something to do with her disappearance?"

"Let me call the family."

Mathews raised an eyebrow. "Not much family left as I hear it."

"Just her stepbrother Bernard. But I'd just like to be the one to tell him," Cash said.

Mathews nodded. "Maybe he'll have some idea how her car ended up down here. But then if he knew his sister was coming down to see you, he would have mentioned it seven years ago, right?"

They'd been over this ground before. "She didn't drive down here to see me. She had plans in Bozeman. But if someone wanted me to look guilty, hiding her car in a barn outside my town would certainly do it."

Mathews nodded in agreement. "Awful lot of trouble to go to since she was living almost five hours away."

"Covering up a murder sometimes requires a lot of trouble, I would imagine," Cash snapped back.

Mathews nodded slowly. "You ought to take a few days off. Didn't I hear that you have a cabin on the other end of the lake?"

Cash said nothing.

"Fishing any good?"

"Smallmouth bass and crappie are biting, a few walleye and northern pike," Cash said, seeing where this was going. "I have some vacation time coming. I think I'll tie up the loose ends back at the office and do that. You have my cell-phone number if you hear anything."

Mathews nodded. "I suppose it is a godsend that her father didn't live to see this." Archie had died five years ago of a heart attack. Jasmine's stepmother Fran was killed just last year in a car accident. "Her stepbrother Bernard is kind of a jackass but I liked the old man and he seemed to like you. He really wanted you to marry his daughter." The investigator sounded a little surprised by that.

No more surprised than Cash, but looking back, Cash knew that was probably why he'd been able to keep his job as sheriff when Jasmine disappeared. Archibald "Archie" Wolfe had never once thought that Cash had anything to do with Jasmine's disappearance.

Cash had expected the prominent and powerful Georgia furniture magnate to hate him on sight the first time they met—just after Jasmine had disappeared. It had seemed impossible that Archibald Wolfe would have ever wanted his Southern belle socialite daughter to marry a small-town sheriff in Montana. Jasmine had already told Cash that her father never liked any of the men she dated.

But Archie had surprised him. "You're the kind of man she needed," the older man had said. "I know she's spoiled and would try a saint's patience, but I think all she needs is the right man to straighten her up."

"Mr. Wolfe, I'm afraid you have it all wrong," Cash had tried to tell him.

"Archie, dammit. You know I disinherited her recently. I would have burned every cent I had to keep her from marrying the likes of Kerrington Landow. But once Jasmine is found and the two of you are married, I'll put her back in my will, you don't need to worry about that."

"I don't want your money, Mr. Wol—Archie, and I don't need it," Cash had said. "Let's just pray Jasmine is found soon."

Archie's eyes had narrowed. He had nodded slowly. "I think you actually mean that. How did my daughter find *you*?"

Cash had shaken his head, thinking that's exactly what Jasmine had done, found him and not the other way around. He'd tried to think of something to say. It hadn't seemed like the time to tell Archie the truth.

Archie had died a broken man, the loss of his daughter more than he could stand.

"Cash? Did you hear what I said?"

He mentally shook himself. "Sorry, John."

Mathews was studying him, frowning. "If there is anything you want to tell me that might come out during this investigation…"

Cash shook his head. How long did he have before he was relieved of his position and his resources taken away so he wouldn't be able to work the case in secret? Not long from Mathews' expression.

"There's nothing I haven't already told you pertaining to the case," Cash answered truthfully.

Mathews nodded slowly, clearly not believing that. "Let me know how the fishing is."

As Cash drove back into town, he knew he'd have to work fast and do his best not to get caught. It was only a matter of time before Mathews learned the truth—and Cash found himself behind bars.

North of Las Vegas, Nevada

THE FEAR DIDN'T REALLY HIT her until Molly lost sight of Vegas in her rearview mirror. She was running for her life and she didn't know where to go or what to do. She had little money and, unlike Vince and Angel who had criminal resources she didn't even want to think about, she had no one to turn to.

She wiped her eyes and straightened, checking the rearview mirror. In this life there isn't time for sentimentality, her father had told her often enough. That was why you didn't get close to anyone. If you cared too much, that person could be used against you. Wasn't that why the Great Maximilian Burke, famous magician and thief, had never let her call him Dad?

He'd insisted she go by Kilpatrick. He'd told her it was her mother's maiden name. Since Max and her mother Lorilee hadn't been married when Molly was born, her name on her birth certificate was Kilpatrick anyway, he'd said.

Molly had asked him once why he and Lorilee hadn't married before her mother died.

"Your mother wouldn't marry me until I got a real job," Max had said with a shrug. "And since I never got a real job…"

Her mother had died when Molly was a baby. She didn't remember her, didn't even have a photograph. Max wasn't the sentimental type. Also, he and Molly were always on the move, so even if there had been photos, they had long been lost.

All she had of her mother was a teddy bear, long worn, that Max had said her mother had given her. The teddy bear had been her most prized possession, but even it had been lost.

She wiped at her tears, tears she shed not for herself but for Lanny. She hadn't let herself think about her father's best friend. Lanny had always been kind to her and had remained Max's friend until her father's death. That was what had gotten Lanny killed, Molly was sure.

Her stomach growled and she realized she hadn't eaten. She pulled off the interstate in one of the tiny, dying towns north of St. George, Utah, and parked in the empty lot of the twenty-four-hour Mom's Home-cooking Café.

A bell jingled over the door as she stepped inside. It was early, but Molly doubted the place was ever hopping. She slid into a cracked vinyl booth and rested her elbows on the cool, worn Formica tabletop.

A skinny gray-haired waitress who looked more tired than even Molly felt, slid a menu and a sweating glass of ice water onto the table. She took a pad and a stubby pencil out of her pocket, leaning on one varicose-veined leg as she waited.

"I'll take the meatloaf special with iced tea, please," Molly said, closing the menu and handing it to her, noticing that the waitress took it without looking at her, pocketed the pad and pencil without writing anything down and left without a word.

Molly watched her go, thinking her own life could be worse. It was a game she and Max used to play.

"You think your situation is bad, kiddo, look at that guy," he would say.

He called her kiddo. She called him Max and had since she was able to talk.

"Better no one knows we're related," he'd always said. "It will be our little secret." He told everyone that he'd picked her up off the street and kept her with him because she made a good assistant for his magic act.

There was a time she'd actually believed he was just trying to protect her by denying their relationship because Maximilian Burke had always been outside the law.

He'd raised her, if a person could call that raising a child. He'd let her come along with him. He used to say, "You're with me, kiddo, I'm not with you." Which meant she didn't get to complain, even when he didn't feed her for several days because he had no money. He would hand her a couple of single-serving-sized packets of peanuts and tell her they would be eating lobster before the week was out.

And they usually were. It had been feast or famine. A transient existence at best. Homeless and hungry at worst. Her father was a second-rate magician but turned out to be a first-class thief.

She glanced out the café window, remembering late nights in greasy-spoon cafés, lying with her head on her arms on the smooth, cool surface of the table, Max waking her when the food was served. Too tired to care, she ate by rote, knowing that tomorrow she might get nothing but peanuts.

"You have to learn to live off your wits," Max used

to say. "It's the best thing I can teach you, kiddo. Some day it will save your life." That day had arrived.

The waitress brought out a plate with a slice of gray-colored meatloaf, instant mashed potatoes with canned brown gravy over them, a large spoonful of canned peas and a stale roll with a pat of margarine.

Molly breathed in the smell first, closing her eyes. This was as close to a mother's home-cooked meal as she'd ever come. What she loved was the familiarity of it. This was home for her, a greasy spoon café in a forgotten town.

She opened her eyes, tears stinging, and picked up her fork, surprised that she still missed Max after all this time. Surprised that she missed him at all. But as much as he'd denied it, he was all the family she'd ever had.

She took a bite of the meatloaf. It was just as the meatloaf she'd known had always tasted, therefore wonderful.

After she'd finished, the waitress brought her a small metal dish with a scoop of ice cream drizzled with chocolate syrup as part of the meatloaf special.

She got up to get the folded newspaper on the counter where the last patron had left it, opened it and read as she ate her ice cream, feeling better if not safer.

The article was on page eight. She wouldn't have even seen it if the photograph of the woman hadn't caught her eye. The spoon halfway to her mouth, the ice cream melting, she read the headline.

Missing Woman's Car Found in Old Barn.

She put down the spoon as she stared at the woman's photograph. The resemblance was uncanny. Looking at the photograph was like looking in a mirror. Or at a ghost. Molly could easily pass for the woman, they looked that much alike.

Heart pounding, Molly read the entire story twice, unable to believe it. Fate had just given her a way out. Her luck had definitely improved.

Las Vegas, Nevada

VINCE WINSLOW PULLED UP in front of the motel room and honked the horn of the large older-model car he'd bought when he'd gotten out of prison.

Vince thought of himself as a fair man. He'd been a mediator in his cell block at prison and everyone agreed he had a way with people. It was a gift. He would hear gripes and grievances, then he would settle them. One way or another. Sometimes he'd just bang a few heads together. Whatever it took.

The one thing he couldn't stand was injustice. It made him violent and that was dangerous for a big, strong man who'd spent most of his fifteen-year stint in the weight room at the prison, planning what to do when he got out.

He honked again and Angel Edwards came out of the motel room scowling at him. Vince slid over to let Angel drive.

"What? Are your legs broken? You can't get out of the car? You got to honk the damned horn?" Angel slid behind the wheel, cursing under his breath.

Compared to Angel, Vince was a saint. Angel was a hothead. Short, wiry, all energy with little brains.

"Haven't you ever wondered why I put up with you?"

Vince asked in his usual soft tone. Right now he was definitely wondering that very thing himself.

Angel snorted. "I'm the best getaway-car driver in the business and you know it."

Vince couldn't argue that. Angel had lightning-fast reflexes. But since that life was behind them, Vince didn't need a getaway driver anymore.

"You also love me," Angel said without looking at him.

Vince stared over at him, realizing that was the only reason he didn't take Angel out into the desert and put a bullet through his brain. Angel was his half brother. Blood was everything, even if your mother had no taste when it came to men.

"Damn, it's like a refrigerator in here," Angel complained, reaching over to turn off the air-conditioning. "You tryin' to kill me?"

All those years of being locked up in the same cell block had made Vince even more aware of his brother's shortcomings. Not that it had ever taken much to set Angel off, but now, once angry, Angel was nearly impossible to control. That had proved to be a problem. On top of that, now that Angel was out of prison, he had unlimited access to sharp instruments and a fifteen-year fixation on getting what he had coming.

"We need to talk," Vince said.

"What is there to talk about?" Angel demanded, glaring over at him. "We find the bitch. We get what's coming to us. This ain't brain surgery."

"My fear is that when we find her, you will go berserk like you did with Lanny and kill her before she tells us what we want to know," Vince pointed out calmly.

"If I hadn't gotten you out of there when I did last night, we would be on death row right now. We almost got caught because you can't control your temper."

"You were going too easy on Lanny. I had him talking. He was just about to tell us. If he had lived just another few seconds…"

Vince groaned. "When we find Molly, you have to refrain from that kind of…persuasion, or we will never get the diamonds."

"If she hasn't already fenced them," Angel snapped.

"She hasn't," Vince said for at least the thousandth time. These particular diamonds couldn't be easily fenced—they were too recognizable. And Vince had his sources on the outside watching for them. There was no way Molly could have tried to fence the uncut stones without him knowing about it.

Angel shifted in the seat, his left cheek twitching from a nervous tic. "Okay, okay. So why are we still sitting here? Let's find the bitch."

"I found her before I found Lanny. She's working at a greasy spoon off the Strip," Vince said.

"You've seen her?" Angel asked, his voice high with excitement and suspicion. "Why didn't you take me with you?"

Vince raised a brow as if to say, "Isn't it obvious?"

"You wouldn't try to cut me out of my share, would you?" Angel asked, going mean on him. Angel didn't trust anyone, but still Vince took it as an insult.

"You're my *brother*." As if that meant anything to Angel. Vince reached into the back seat and picked up the latest in laptop computers. Opening it, he booted it up.

"What? You going to check your e-mail?" Angel snapped.

"Patience. She isn't going to get away," Vince told him calmly. "I put a global positioning device on her car."

"What?" Angel swore. "You were close enough to her to put some damned gadget on her car but you didn't grab her? Are you crazy?"

"Like a fox," Vince said.

"So where is she, Mr. Smart Guy?"

Vince studied the screen and smiled. "She's running for her life."

Chapter Three

When Cash got back to his office, he found his sister Dusty sitting behind his desk. She leaped to her feet like the teenager she was and ran to him, throwing her arms around his neck.

"Did they find her?" she asked stepping back from the quick hug, a mixture of hope and fear in her expression.

He shook his head and stepped around behind his desk.

Dusty was dressed in her usual jeans, western shirt, boots and a straw cowboy hat pulled low. A single blond braid trailed down her slim back. She was a beauty, although she seemed to do everything possible to hide the fact that she was female. Cash wasn't sure if it was because Dusty was raised pretty much in an all male household or because she actually loved working on the ranch more than doing girl stuff.

"You're going to keep looking though, aren't you?" She sounded surprised he was here rather than out with the other officers searching the Trayton place.

"I'm off the case, Dusty," he said dropping into his chair. His sister had been only eleven when Jasmine disappeared. He doubted she understood the implications of Jasmine's car being found so close to town, but she would soon enough, once the Antelope Flats rumor mill kicked in. He wanted to be the one to tell her, but still the words came hard.

"I was her—" he paused, the word coming hard "—fiancée and with her car found near here, I'm a suspect in her homicide." He waved a hand through the air, knowing there was more that would come out but no reason to open that can of worms until he had to.

"Homicide?"

"A sufficient amount of her blood type was found in the car to change her disappearance to a probable homicide," he said.

"How could anyone think *you* would hurt her?" Dusty cried. "She was the love of your life—*is* the love of your life. She can't be dead. She's probably in Europe just like you thought. She'll come back once she hears about her car being found and, when she sees you again, she'll remember what you shared and she'll be sorry she stayed away and she won't ever leave again."

He smiled up at her, surprised that his tomboy sister was such a romantic and touched that she cared so much. He didn't have the heart to tell her how wrong she was. "What are you doing in town? I thought you were helping with branding?"

"Shelby sent me in to check on you and tell you that you're expected at dinner tomorrow night." Dusty rolled her eyes. "Who knows what big bombshell she's planning to drop now."

Shelby was their mother, but it was complicated as all hell. Just a few months ago, out of the blue, Shelby Ward McCall had shown up at the ranch. What made that unusual was that Cash thought his mother had died when he was just over a year old.

Shelby had not only announced that she was alive, but that she and their father Asa had cooked up her demise. It seemed they had thought it would be better for Cash and his three brothers to believe she had died rather than just left. Shelby and Asa couldn't live with each other and didn't want the children to have the stigma of divorce hanging over them.

At least that was their story and they were sticking to it. But to make matters worse, he and his brothers had always thought that their little sister Dusty was the result of an affair their father had nineteen years ago. Asa had brought Dusty home when she was a baby with some cock-and-bull story about her being orphaned. He'd legally adopted her and Cash guessed he thought his sons didn't notice how much she looked like them.

Turned out that Dusty was the result of Asa and Shelby getting together years ago in secret to "discuss" things.

Well, now Shelby was back at the ranch and tongues were wagging in four counties. Cash was trying to keep both of his parents from going to prison for fraud and Dusty was hardly speaking to either parent.

His family had always been the talk of the town for one reason or another. Cash knew that was partly why he'd become sheriff. He was tired of being one of the wild McCall boys.

"Say you will come to dinner," Dusty pleaded. Dusty had taken the betrayal the hardest. It didn't help that she looked so much like her mother. She'd also been the closest to their father and felt betrayed by him. But she was especially angry with her mother. While Dusty could possibly understand how Shelby might walk away from four sons, she couldn't forgive her mother for giving up a daughter.

Since Shelby's astonishing reappearance, the family undercurrents were deadly. She never had explained why she'd returned to the living. But it was obvious a lot more was going on between her and Asa than either had let on. Cash had seen the looks that had passed between them, seen Shelby crying and Asa hadn't been himself since she'd come back. Their father, a cantankerous, stubborn, almost seventy-year-old man who'd alienated all four of his sons on a regular basis, was actually trying to be nice.

It worried the hell out of Cash.

So it was no wonder that the last thing he wanted to do was attend one of the McCalls' famous knock-down-drag-out family dinners—especially now.

But he knew that an invitation to a family dinner was really a summons to appear. If he sent word back that he wasn't coming, Shelby herself would drive into town to try to change his mind. He didn't need that.

"I'll be there." He hated to think what new surprises might be sprung at dinner tomorrow night.

Dusty sighed in relief at his acceptance. "I think the

dinner is probably about Brandon. You know he's been acting weird lately."

Cash had noticed a change in his brother, but didn't think it weird. Brandon, at thirty-three, seemed to have finally grown up. He'd taken on more responsibility out at the ranch, had really seemed to have settled down. He was talking about attending law school next fall and, according to their older brother J.T., had opened an account at the bank to save for it. "Isn't it about time Brandon grew up?"

Dusty didn't seem to be listening. "He comes in really late at night. I think he has a girlfriend, but he denies it."

Cash laughed. "If you're right, he'll tell us when he's ready."

She made a face at the "if you're right" part. It was a given that a McCall was always right, especially a female one. "Aren't you even curious why he would try to keep a girlfriend secret?"

"No, we're a family of secrets," Cash said, realizing just how true that was. He thought of his own secret, pushed for years into some dark corner of his heart.

The problem with secrets was that they didn't stay that way. It was only a matter of time, now that Jasmine's car had been found, before his came out.

Somewhere outside St. George, Utah

AFTER LEAVING THE CAFÉ, Molly found a newspaper stand and bought a copy of the paper. She ripped out the article and sat behind the wheel of her car, studying the photograph of the missing woman.

On closer inspection, the woman didn't look that much like her. The resemblance was in the shape of the face, the spacing and color of the eyes, the generous mouth. The hair was different, long, straight and white-blond compared to Molly's curly, short, darker blond locks.

But with some makeup, a few highlights in her hair and the right clothes… The clincher was that the woman was close to her age—just a year and a half older—and about her height—an inch taller and ten pounds heavier.

As Molly looked into the woman's face, she felt a chill at just the thought of what she was thinking of doing. Talk about bad karma.

According to the article, Jasmine Wolfe was last seen at a gas station on the outskirts of Bozeman seven years ago. The clerk at the station had noticed a man approach the blond woman driving the new red sports car. The man was about average height wearing a dark jacket, jeans and cap. The clerk didn't see his face or note his hair color.

When the clerk had looked up again, the man was holding the woman's arm and the two were getting into the car. They appeared to be arguing. The clerk hadn't thought much about it, just assumed they were together, until she'd read about the search for the missing woman and remembered Jasmine, the new red sports car and witnessing the incident.

It was speculated that Jasmine had been abducted by an unknown assailant who had forced her into her car at possibly knife- or gunpoint. That theory was heightened a month later when a man was arrested outside of Bozeman trying to abduct a woman at another gas station in the same area.

The man was sent to prison and, while he never admitted to abducting Jasmine Wolfe, he was believed to have been involved in several other missing persons' cases in the area, including hers. The man had committed a murder in prison and was still serving time there with little chance of parole.

That was good news. But not as good news as who Jasmine Wolfe was—the daughter of Archibald Wolfe, a furniture magnate from Atlanta, Georgia. Archie, as he was known to his friends and employees, had offered a sizable reward for any information about his daughter. The reward had never been collected.

Molly let out a low whistle. "You've just hit the jackpot, kiddo," Max would have said. "All you have to do is convince the sheriff that you're the missing woman, then the family will be a snap. Seven years. People change a lot in seven years."

Maybe, she thought. But Antelope Flats Sheriff Cash McCall would definitely be the one she'd have to fool. Jasmine had been engaged to him, according to the newspaper. A man would know his former fiancée. Except if she kept him at arm's length, which shouldn't be that hard to do. There was no photograph of the sheriff but Molly could just imagine some backwoods local yokel.

She reached into the back seat for her old road atlas. Antelope Flats, Montana, was on the southeastern corner of the state just miles from the Wyoming border. Bozeman, where Jasmine Wolfe had been a graduate student at Montana State University, looked to be a good five hours away.

Antelope Flats had to be tiny, really tiny, since it appeared to be no more than a dot on the map.

No one would ever look for Molly there. Especially if she were someone else altogether. She knew she'd go crazy within a week in a place like that. But a week might be long enough.

Molly's original plan had been to run, just keep one step ahead of Vince and Angel. But as she stared at Jasmine Wolfe's photograph, she knew this plan—bad karma and all— was her best bet.

She opened the container she'd brought from the café. Chocolate-cream pie. It was about as homemade as the rest of the meal had been, but just as familiar.

And, she thought taking a big bite of the pie, she would need to put on a few pounds if she was going to Antelope Flats, Montana. She could do a lot with makeup, a change in her hair color and style. She could become Jasmine Wolfe, she was sure of it.

But what if Jasmine Wolfe's body turned up. State investigators were searching the abandoned farm. Or even Jasmine herself, alive and in the flesh after seeing the article? And even if neither happened, still Molly would have to pull off a major magic act with the sheriff.

But, no thanks to her father, Molly had been performing from the time she could walk. And like her father, she'd always believed in omens as well as in luck. Just when she had two killers after her and needed a place to disappear, she'd seen this article. If that wasn't a sign, she didn't know what was.

Also, she was a realist. She had only a little money saved. It wouldn't last long. If she hoped to stay alive, what better way than becoming someone else for a short period of time?

She wasn't worried about Vince and Angel seeing the article and putting two and two together. Even if they could add—or read—she doubted either had ever read a newspaper in their lives.

If by chance Vince and Angel saw the story in a newspaper, she didn't think they would notice the resemblance between Jasmine Wolfe and her. Neither man had seen her since she was fourteen and she'd changed a lot. And while she thought her resemblance to the missing woman was uncanny—it was the little touches she would make in her appearance that would convince others she was Jasmine.

Going to a pay phone, she made another anonymous call to the Vegas Police Department. Vince and Angel hadn't been picked up yet. But someone else had called in and given a description of a car leaving the scene of the murder.

She gave a description of each man as if she'd seen them leaving the murder scene as well. She told them that she'd heard the big one call the little one Angel, the one who looked like he had a prison tattoo on his neck.

It shouldn't take long for the police to put it all together. The day Max, Vince and Angel had pulled off the big heist in Hollywood, they'd returned to Lanny's house where Lanny and Molly had been waiting. It was there that the police had arrested Vince and Angel. It was there that Max had shown up in a separate vehicle and, seeing the police, had tried to make a run for it and was shot down in the street.

Molly tried not to think about that day, about her father dying in her arms in the middle of the street.

As she hung up the phone, she didn't kid herself. It

could take a while before the two recently paroled felons were caught. Once they were, she was sure the police would find something on the two to send them both back to prison—even if it couldn't be proved that Vince and Angel had killed Lanny.

Still, her best bet was to stall for time.

Hiding was always preferable to running. With luck, she could pull this off. And if she played her cards right, there could even be some money in it. She cringed at how much she sounded like Max. But taking money from Jasmine's family was no worse than pretending to be her, was it?

And if anyone could pass herself off as someone else, it was Molly Kilpatrick. She'd pretended to be someone else for so many years that she had no idea who the real Molly Kilpatrick was anymore.

The decision made, she folded up the clipping and put it in her purse. She would follow the story as she headed to Montana. There was always the chance that Jasmine Wolfe would turn up before she got there.

Meanwhile, she had a few tricks up her sleeve, thanks to her father the Great Maximilian Burke, magician and thief.

Antelope Flats, Montana

CASH PICKED UP THE PHONE the moment Dusty left and dialed Bernard Wolfe's number. Bernard was about Cash's age, thirty-five, four inches shorter, stocky like a weight lifter, with rust-colored hair, small dark brown eyes and a cocky arrogance that seemed to come with the Wolfe fortune. Cash had disliked Bernard from the get-go and vice versa.

"She's just playing you to drive our father crazy," Bernard had said to him when they'd met for the first time. "It's what she does. Plays with people. Our father cut off her money so now she's going to make him pay by threatening to marry you. You are one of many in a long line. She'll tire of you and this game—if she hasn't already."

It had taken all of Cash's control not to slug him.

After Jasmine's disappearance and Archie's death, Bernard had taken over the furniture conglomerate, a business that had put him in the top five hundred of the nation's wealthiest men.

"Wolfe residence," a man with a distinct English accent answered.

Cash made a face and told himself he shouldn't have been surprised that Bernard would have an English butler.

"I'm calling for Mr. Wolfe. My name is Sheriff Cash McCall of Antelope Flats, Montana. Would you please tell him it's important. It has to do with his sister—step-sister," he corrected. "Jasmine."

As sheriff of the county, he'd had to make a lot of calls like this, some worse than others. They were never easy. He wondered how Bernard would take the news. Did Bernard even give a thought to his missing stepsister?

"Yes?" Bernard said when he came on the line a moment later. "What is this about?" He had only a touch of cultured Southern drawl, unlike his father. Bernard was Oxford educated, that probably explained it.

Cash had not talked to him in almost seven years. He

cleared his throat. "This is Sheriff Cash McCall. I want-ed to let you know that Jasmine's car's been found."

Silence, then what sounded like Bernard pulling up a chair and sitting down. "Where?"

"Just a few miles from Antelope Flats. The car was discovered in an old abandoned barn on a deserted farm north of the lake. It had been covered with a tarp."

"Was Jasmine…?"

"No." Cash waited to hear relief in Bernard's voice but heard nothing. "The investigators are searching the farm. They found blood and are treating the case as a homicide."

"They aren't letting you near the case I hope."

Cash clamped down his jaw, then took a breath and let it out. "I wanted to be the one to call you."

"Why is that?"

"Personal and professional courtesy. It's often hard on family members to get this kind of news."

Bernard made a rude sound. "I'll fly out as soon as I can." He hung up.

Cash stared at the phone in his hand. What had he ex-pected? He wasn't sure. There was no doubt that he'd hoped to rattle Bernard, shake him up a little, maybe even get him to make a mistake when it came to his sto-ry from seven years before.

Bernard had said he'd been hiking up in the Bridger Mountains the day Jasmine disappeared. His alibi was his friend and Jasmine's former fiancée Kerrington Landow. Supposedly the two had been together, which provided them both with alibis.

Cash had always suspected that the man the clerk had

seen with Jasmine at the gas station was Bernard. He fit
the description—just like the man who'd been arrested
for an attempted abduction in the same area. A man who
had refused to confess to Jasmine's abduction even
when offered a deal.

As Cash hung up the phone, he knew Bernard would
call Kerrington and tell him about Jasmine's car being
found. Cash had heard that Kerrington had married Jasmine's best friend and former roommate, Sandra Perkins.

After seven years and marriage to another woman,
what would Kerrington do? Come to Antelope Flats?
Cash wouldn't be surprised. Kerrington and Bernard
were both so deep in Jasmine's disappearance that neither would be able to stay away.

Somewhere south of Montana

MOLLY STOPPED at a computer store and used the Inter-
net service to access everything she could find about
Jasmine Wolfe and her disappearance. Because of her
prominent old Southern family, the story had been in all
the major newspapers.

Molly read every article she could find, becoming
more excited as she did. This could definitely be the answer to her problems.

The sheriff was the drawback though. That and the
fact that Molly hadn't pulled any kind of "magic trick"
since her father had died fifteen years before. She'd
given up that way of life and had promised herself that
she would never go back to it.

For years she'd never stayed in one place long, know-

ing that Vince and Angel could get out on parole at any
time. At least that's what she told herself. In truth, the
one thing she hadn't been able to cast off was the transient lifestyle of her childhood or the fear that Max had
been right—that fraud was in her blood.

No matter how hard she tried, she found she got restless within weeks and would quit her job, move somewhere else and get another mediocre job. Fortunately
she had an assortment of skills that lent themselves to
quick employment and she'd never been looking for a
"good" job since she'd be moving on soon anyway.

But Vince and Angel were out of prison now and after her. She hadn't seen anything in the papers about
Lanny Giliano. She could only assume he was dead and
she was next. She had to do a disappearing act, and maybe Max was right. Maybe fraud was in her blood and
just waiting to come out.

On a hunch, she found an online video of Jasmine
giving a speech at some charity benefit. The father had
put the video online at the time of Jasmine's disappearance, saying he thought his daughter might be suffering from amnesia and hoped someone would recognize
her and call.

Molly watched the video a half dozen times online
until she could mimic Jasmine's gestures, her way of
speaking, her facial expressions. Mimicking was something Molly had learned at an early age, a gimmick she
and her father used during his act when he pretended to
read minds in the audience.

Molly would secretly pick someone from the audience while her father had his back turned. Then he

would read her mind and point to the person she'd picked. It amazed the audience. But the trick had been quite simple. She would just mimic the expression and body language of the person and her father would spot it and match it with the right person. Magic!

It amazed her how quickly all that training came back. Her mind was already working out the details. Not that she wasn't aware of the danger. Identity fraud. Fortunately, there was little record of her life the past fifteen years since her father's death or, for that matter, the fourteen years before that.

All of her "jobs" with her father hadn't involved paperwork, and few of her jobs had since. She preferred work where she was paid "off the books" in cash. Jobs where she didn't have to provide a social security number or an address. Much safer.

And there were enough employers who wanted to avoid paying taxes that it hadn't been hard to find menial work. She had pretty much remained invisible over those years, but she knew that wouldn't protect her from Vince and Angel. They would turn over every rock to find her. And they wouldn't stop until they did.

The way Molly saw it, only one person—the person who put Jasmine's car in that barn—would know that she really wasn't Jasmine. And that person was in prison serving time for his other crimes.

Which was good, since Molly already had two killers looking for her. That was sufficient.

Chapter Four

Atlanta, Georgia

Kerrington Landow never thought he'd be relieved to have the phone ring in the middle of a meal. But if he had to listen to one more of Sandra's lies…

"Let the maid get it," Sandra said with impatience.

He ignored her as he shoved back his chair and gave her one of his this-isn't-over-by-a-long-shot glares. Throwing down his napkin, he turned and stalked out of the dining room to take the call on the hall phone.

"Hello," he snapped, surprised how furious he was. In truth, he didn't care if Sandra was cheating on him or not. No, what made him angry was that she seemed to think he was so stupid he didn't know what she was up to.

"Jasmine's car's been found."

He went rigid.

"Did you hear me?" Bernard Wolfe demanded.

"Yes. I heard you." But still he couldn't believe… "What about—?" He looked up. Sandra had followed him. She was watching him from the dining room doorway, frowning, definitely interested in whom he was talking to.

"They haven't found Jasmine's body. Not yet anyway," Bernard was saying. He sounded upset.

The same way Sandra would be when she heard. He had purposely not said Jasmine's name in front of her for that very reason. Sandra had thrown Jasmine up to him for years.

"I know I was your second choice," she said whenever they had a fight. "Do you have any idea what it's like living in that woman's shadow? It was bad enough when Jasmine was alive. But now I have to contend with her ghost?"

He had tried to reassure Sandra but the truth was, he'd never gotten over Jasmine and doubted he ever would. And now her car had been found.

"What is it?" Sandra asked coming down the hall. She was looking at him as if she'd seen him pale, had noticed the tremor in his hand clutching the phone. Sweat broke out under his arms. He worried she could smell the fear on him.

"They found her car in an old barn near Antelope Flats," Bernard was saying on the other end of the line.

Kerrington said nothing. He'd checked out the town when Jasmine had told him her plans to marry the sheriff. He'd laughed in her face. He'd known she would never go through with it.

"What?" Sandra demanded. She was standing directly in front of him now, her eyes locked on his face as if she could see through him, always had been able to.

Sometimes he forgot that Sandra had known Jasmine probably as well as anyone. She and mousy little Patty Franklin had been Jasmine's roommates at Montana State University in Bozeman. Jasmine had gone there on a whim after she'd already worked her way through all the men at several other universities, he thought bitterly.

Sandra had been the opposite of Jasmine, tall and slender, her hair dark like her eyes. She'd been available and he'd needed someone to use to make Jasmine jealous. Jasmine would never have believed it if he'd dated Patty the Pathetic, as Bernard called her.

"What?" Sandra demanded again, practically spitting in his face.

"They've found Jasmine's car," he said, knowing it would be impossible to keep something like this from her.

He'd expected the green-eyed monster to rear her ugly head. Instead, Sandra seemed stunned. She leaned against the wall, her face stony and remote.

"Sandra is there?" Bernard said with obvious disgust.

Where else had Bernard expected her to be? She was his wife, although Kerrington couldn't even guess where she'd been spending a lot of her time lately. He was hit with the most ridiculous thought. That the man Sandra had been seeing behind his back was Bernard. The two deserved each other, no doubt about that. But they couldn't stand to be in the same room together.

He rubbed a hand over his face and turned his back to Sandra to look in the hall mirror. He felt a need to assure himself and he'd always been reassured by what he saw in the mirror, as long as he didn't look too deeply.

Jasmine used to say he was classically tall, dark and

handsome. Only she'd made it sound as if he were a cliché. He'd even overheard her and her brother Bernard refer to him as her "mindless pretty boy."

He shook off the memory, replacing it with a more pleasant one. Jasmine naked and in his arms begging for more.

"I'm flying out tonight," Bernard was saying. "I think you and I should talk before I go, don't you? The cops are going to be asking a lot more questions. I think we need to get our stories straight so we tell them the same thing we did seven years ago."

Kerrington swore softly under his breath. It had been so long, he'd thought all of this was behind them. He should have known Jasmine's car would eventually turn up. Wasn't that what he'd hoped? Just not now, not after all this time.

"I'm going, too," he whispered into the phone as he caught movement out of the corner of his eye. Sandra had gone into the living room and sat down, her sour hatred of Jasmine almost palpable.

"You should just stay home and take care of your wife," Bernard said.

"Never mind what I should do," Kerrington growled. Had Bernard heard something about Sandra? Is that why he was suggesting Kerrington take care of his wife? Or was that earlier thought of Bernard and Sandra closer to the truth than he'd wanted to admit? It would be just like Bernard.

"I'm flying to Montana as soon as I can get a flight," Kerrington said, keeping his voice down, his back to Sandra and the living room. "We can talk there."

"That's not a smart thing to do."

"She was my girlfriend," Kerrington argued.

"The one who *dumped* you."

"Who knows who she'd be married to now if she were still alive."

Bernard made a scoffing sound on the other end of the line. "Assuming she's dead." He hung up.

Assuming she's dead. Kerrington stood holding the phone. Did Bernard know something? It had been Bernard who'd come to him with the offer of an alibi.

"If you need to, you can say you were with me," Bernard had said two days after Jasmine disappeared— just before the cops arrived to question them. "I was hiking in the Bridger Mountains. Took my gear and camped up there. Didn't get back home until well after dark the second day."

Kerrington had been so grateful to have an alibi at all that he'd gone along with Bernard's. It wasn't until later that he realized he'd also given Bernard an alibi.

He hung up the phone, then turned, bracing himself for the mother of all arguments he knew he was about to have with Sandra.

But Sandra was gone.

Antelope Flats, Montana

NEWS TRAVELED AT the speed of light, even in a county where there was little or no cell-phone service and ranches were miles apart.

The news about Jasmine's car being found had given Shelby McCall's return-from-the-dead story a rest.

For hours Cash had been able to avoid his mother's call, but when the phone rang shortly after he'd hung up from talking to Bernard Wolfe, he knew before he answered who was calling.

"Cash? Are you all right?"

He wanted to laugh. He was so far from all right.... "I'm fine."

"I think you should move back home so you are close to your family during this time."

That did make him laugh. This coming from a woman who'd been gone for thirty years? Where was his mother when he'd needed advice about Jasmine? Being raised in an all-male household had left him pretty clueless about women. Dusty hadn't counted since she was just a kid. He really could have used a mother during those years.

"I'm sorry, Cash."

Sorry that Jasmine's car had been found and searchers expected to find her body in some shallow grave on the old farm at any time? Or sorry that she'd never been a mother to him and it was too late to start now?

"I know what you must be going through."

"Do you?" he said, then could have kicked himself.

"Obviously you loved her or you wouldn't have asked her to marry you."

He said nothing, afraid of what would come out.

"Let me know if there is anything I can do." She seemed to be waiting for him to say something. When he didn't, she hung up. She didn't mention dinner. Must have realized it would have been a bad time to ask for anything.

When he looked up, his brother J.T. was standing in his office doorway.

"Mother? She means well," J.T. said, closing the door behind him as he came in.

Cash grunted.

J.T. stood, looking uncomfortable. That was the problem with being raised by a bad-tempered man like Asa and a disagreeable ranch foreman like Buck. The brothers had grown up believing that softness was a weakness. So they sure as hell knew nothing about comforting each other.

Even Dusty was more tomboy than girl.

But J.T.'s rough edges had been smoothed a lot since Regina Holland had come into his life last fall. Cash had seen the change in him and approved. Reggie, as J.T. called her, was perfect for his brother, strong and yet soft in all the right ways. She was like a ray of sunshine in J.T.'s life and it showed in his older brother's face. Cash had never seen J.T. so happy.

"Is there anything I can do?" he asked now.

Cash shook his head, figuring Reggie had sent him. "The state investigators took over the search. I'm supposed to go fishing."

J.T. nodded. "You're not going to though, are you?"

Cash smiled. His brother knew him too well.

"Reggie said if you need someone to talk to…"

Cash laughed. He *knew* Reggie had sent J.T. His brother looked too uncomfortable for words. "Tell her thank you."

J.T. nodded, looked down at his boots, then up at Cash. "I'm sorry."

Cash nodded. "Maybe it will finally be over." He knew that was what his family had hoped for, that he'd be able to move on once he knew what had happened to Jasmine. If they only knew the truth. He feared though that before this investigation was over, they *would* know. Everyone would.

After J.T. left, Cash picked up the phone and dialed the number for Jasmine's car insurance company, which he'd found in her glove box. He knew Mathews would find out soon enough that he was doing some investigating on his own and all hell would break loose.

But all hell was going to break loose eventually anyway and he couldn't just wait for the state boys to call and tell him they'd found Jasmine's body and they had some questions for him.

Atlanta, Georgia

BERNARD WENT THROUGH the motions. He called to have the company jet readied, instructed George, his English butler, to pack for him, and told the chauffeur to stand by to take him to the private airstrip later tonight.

Bernard had held it together fairly well he thought. Even when he'd had to deal with that jackass Kerrington. It was just like the fool to fly to Montana.

But he'd wanted to be the one to tell him. He didn't want Kerrington seeing it on the news and doing something stupid. And it would be hitting the news, if it hadn't already. He seldom paid any attention to more than the financial news.

He thought about ringing George and having the bottle of champagne he'd asked to be chilled brought out and opened. But he could wait.

He'd waited seven years so he could have Jasmine declared legally dead. Before their father had died, Archie had put aside part of his estate for Jasmine, still holding onto the ridiculous hope that she would turn up one day.

Bernard deserved that money. He'd spent his life "watching out" for his stepsister. "Keep an eye on her, won't you, Bernard," Archibald Wolfe would say. "Take care of your sister."

He wished he had a dollar for every time he'd heard his stepfather say those words.

His mother had married Archie when Bernard was four. Jasmine had been just a baby, her mother having died in childbirth.

Bernard had seen his stepfather struggle with trying to love him as much as he did Jasmine. There had been times when Bernard had felt loved, felt like he really was a Wolfe, not just adopted because his mother had married Archie.

But then Jasmine had grown up, been a wild teenager and an even wilder adult. Keeping her out of trouble had proved impossible. She had loved to upset their father, hadn't cared that she got Bernard and herself into trouble, had rebelled at every turn as if it were her birthright. The Wolfe money had meant nothing to her. She was Daddy's golden girl and she'd known he would never disinherit her. At least not for long.

Bernard had never felt that secure as the stepson.

When Jasmine had decided to get another degree in a long line of degrees, this time in Montana, Archie had asked Bernard to go with her. "Just keep an eye on her. Make sure she's all right. Be there if she needs you."

Bernard had wanted to laugh. Jasmine hadn't needed him, hadn't even liked him, and he'd resented the hell
out of his role as protector of his precious stepsister.

But Bernard had known he'd had no option. Archie
had set him up in a condo near the university with unlimited spending and nothing really to do other than ski and
party—and of course try to keep Jasmine out of trouble.

Jasmine had reverted to form and had enticed Kerrington to come to Montana so they could be together, except for those times when she was bored with him. Archie
had heard about it and had been furious with Bernard, but
even more furious with Jasmine. This time Archie had
done more than threaten to disinherit her, he had done it.

Kerrington had been beside himself, begging Jasmine
to make up with her father. He and Jasmine had argued
and the next thing Bernard knew, she had announced that
she was engaged to some cowboy sheriff from Antelope
Flats, Montana. Kerrington had been inconsolable. He'd
been dating Jasmine's roommate Sandra to make Jasmine jealous. It apparently hadn't worked.

Bernard had pretended to reason with his sister, but
with her out of the will, he would get everything. Jasmine had never listened to him anyway. He hoped she
would marry her cowboy sheriff and live in some din-
ky town in Montana, but he knew her better than that.
Jasmine had just been playing them all.

Then Jasmine had disappeared. Archie had never
said outright that he blamed Bernard, but Bernard knew
he did. It had taken a while, but Bernard had finally gotten close to his stepfather before Archie died.

He'd worked hard to take over the Wolfe Furniture

conglomerate, proven himself worthy in so many ways. In the end, he'd felt as if Archie respected him, maybe even loved him. Then Archie had died and Bernard's mother Fran had been killed.

Bernard was left alone—with everything—except for the chunk that had been left to Jasmine.

In just a few weeks, Bernard could have had her declared legally dead. And now this. Jasmine's car turning up, stirring it all up again. It was as if Jasmine was plotting against him from the grave. As if she couldn't stand for him to be happy.

Now he would have to fly to Montana or it would look suspicious. He would have to act as if he gave a damn. He just hoped it wouldn't take long. He'd always resented Jasmine, often disliked her. But right now he hated her.

His cell phone played "Dixie" in his suit pocket. He didn't have to look at the number to know whom it was. He also knew what she would want. "Yes?"

"I need to see you. Where are you?"

"At home getting ready to leave for Montana." He'd been waiting for her call. Had the champagne chilling for the two of them.

"Don't move." She hung up.

He smiled and snapped his phone shut as he thought of her and what she would want him to do to her. It was warped, twisted in ways he didn't even want to think about. It was also dangerous. But worth it.

He checked to make sure George was finished with his packing, then rang the kitchen and asked for the champagne to be brought up to the master bedroom.

She would be here soon. He was already aroused

just thinking about the pain he would inflict on her. Maybe this wouldn't be such a bad day after all.

Las Vegas, Nevada

"ARE YOU CRAZY?" Angel demanded for the hundredth time. "You let Molly get away."

"She knows we're after her," Vince assured him again. "I was counting on Lanny calling her. She'll lead us right to the diamonds. It's all part of my plan."

"You'd better hope this works," Angel said.

Vince heard the threat in his brother's tone. "I thought you might like to gamble while I get everything ready before we go after her."

Angel's eyes lit because he knew Vince would also provide the money. Angel had already blown what little he'd had.

Four hours later, Vince found Angel at a blackjack table in the casino where he'd left him earlier. From Angel's expression, he'd lost all the money Vince had given him and was in a foul mood. Nothing new there.

"Come on," Vince said.

"I hope to hell we're finally going to do something," Angel snapped as they left the casino and headed for the car. "I'm sick of waiting around."

Vince slid into the passenger seat as Angel got behind the wheel. He sat tapping the steering wheel as if he couldn't sit still. With each passing day, Angel had become more tense. Sitting next to him was like being next to an electrical wire in a thunderstorm. Vince wasn't sure how much longer he could keep Angel under control.

"I told you. We needed to give her a head start," Vince said, knowing this wasn't what Angel wanted to hear.

Angel swore as he pulled out of the casino parking lot in a screech of tires. He pushed his foot hard onto the gas pedal and roared out into the traffic.

"We've waited fifteen years," Vince said patiently. "We can wait a little longer. She's still moving. I want to wait until she lights."

Angel shot him a look and almost rear-ended the car in front of them. He slammed on the brakes. "Did you ever consider that she's gotten rid of the car and you're tracking the wrong person?"

"She won't get rid of the car. She has no reason to."

"You should have let me handle it," Angel argued. "If you'd let me wait for her outside the café where she worked it would be over by now."

Vince didn't doubt that. "Like you handled Lanny? You would have killed her before we found out where the diamonds were and where would that've left us?"

"You've never given me enough credit," Angel complained, slamming his fist down on the steering wheel as the traffic began to move again. "You think I couldn't do this without you?"

Vince felt himself go cold.

Angel seemed to calm down. "You're sure this GPS thing will work, we'll be able to find her?"

"Global positioning system."

"I know what the hell it is," Angel snapped. "I just don't like the idea that she's taken off and we might not be able to find her again."

"We can pinpoint her location down to the street number," Vince said. "Once she stops running, I can even request a map to show us exactly how to get there." He could see that Angel was dubious. Angel hadn't been interested in learning about computers or the new electronics while in prison.

"She thinks she's gotten away, that she's safe. That's why I don't want to crowd her."

Angel muttered something under his breath.

Vince groaned and glanced in his side mirror. "We agreed we would do this together," he said to Angel as he felt a headache coming on. "Or we don't do it at all."

Angel shot him a look. "What the hell is that supposed to mean?"

Vince didn't answer. He spotted a black-and-white behind him, the patrol-car light bar gleaming in the desert sun. Vince glanced over at the speedometer then up the street. "Watch your speed."

Vince figured he would have to give Angel more money to lose gambling. It would be the only way to keep his brother from getting into trouble while they waited.

Angel let up on the gas. They cruised through the intersection.

Vince looked in the side mirror again. The cop in the patrol car had pulled in two cars behind them. Vince looked ahead and saw another cop car turn into the motel where he and Angel had been staying.

"Trouble," he said as yet another patrol car fell in behind them.

"What?"

"We've been made," Vince said.

Angel's gaze darted up to the rearview mirror.

"Another car just turned into our motel," Vince said.

Angel swore. "Who would put the cops on us?"

"Who do you think?"

As Angel drove on past their motel, Vince saw yet another patrol car coming toward them. The cop hit his brakes. "They know our car. He's spotted us."

The cop made a U-turn in the middle of the street, flashing lights and siren coming on.

Angel hit the gas and ran the next red light. Brakes screeched, horns blared and a wail of police sirens took up the cry behind them. Vince was glad Angel was behind the wheel. Angel loved this. He cornered hard and accelerated, driving Vince back against the seat.

So Molly wanted to play hardball? Vince was surprised. He still thought of her as a fourteen-year-old little girl. This changed his perception of her.

Another cop car joined in the chase and Vince thought he heard a helicopter overhead. As Angel wheeled around corners, racing along the backstreets of Vegas to the scream of sirens, Vince shook his head. He was not pleased with Molly. How could she call the cops on them after it had been cops who'd killed Max, the man who had picked her up off the street and been like a father to her? Did the woman have no loyalty at all?

He sighed, unable to understand that kind of thinking. He had planned to cut Molly some slack in respect for Max. He might have even let her live after she gave them the jewels. Or at least he would have told Angel to kill her quickly.

But now she'd left him little option. He would let Angel use the knife on her, keeping her alive until she gave them the jewels and apologized for betraying them.

First though, they had to escape the cops. Then there would be no more waiting. They were going after Molly.

Atlanta, Georgia

KERRINGTON POURED HIMSELF a stiff drink and sat down in his empty living room. He couldn't believe Sandra had left without a word—not after they'd just been arguing about her recent disappearances.

He'd checked the garage, not surprised to find her car gone. She wasn't even trying to hide her affair. Did she really believe he was going to put up with this? The woman must think him a complete fool.

He took a gulp of his drink. The expensive Scotch sent a wave of warmth through him. A thought floated past on the boozy warmth. What if it wasn't an affair? He couldn't imagine what else Sandra would be sneaking behind his back about if not sleeping around. He realized he had no idea what she did all day. Or with whom.

He finished the drink and poured himself another, the booze calming him. He was almost relieved Sandra had left. She would have been looking for a fight if she'd stayed.

"What do you care if Jasmine's car's been found?" she would have demanded. "Like she gave a damn about you." Sandra always threw it up to him that Jasmine had broken the engagement.

"She *dumped* you," Sandra was fond of reminding

him. "After that big article on the society page. How did that make you feel?"

Sick. But he'd never told Sandra that. Sandra thought he had been embarrassed, made to feel like a fool. What Sandra didn't know was that when you lost someone like Jasmine all you thought about was getting her back. Once you got over the initial shock and that feeling of being sick to your stomach.

Jasmine had a way of making nothing matter but her. She was like a drug you needed to survive. You would do anything to have her.

Unfortunately, Jasmine knew it. She made you crazy, until you felt that if you couldn't have her, no one else would either. Hell, he'd followed her to Montana and she would have changed her mind and married him if it hadn't been for her father cutting her out of the will.

He sipped his drink, eyes narrowing at the thought of Jasmine. If she were alive, she would have come to her senses and realized he was the only man for her. How different his life would have been. Her father would have come around. Archie would have never denied Jasmine her legacy if he truly believed she had married the right man. And Kerrington was the right man.

And he would never have married Sandra. Even when she told him she was pregnant with his baby. She blamed Jasmine's disappearance for her miscarriage. Bernard had always said Sandra wasn't even pregnant and Kerrington had been a fool to buy in to her story without demanding proof.

All water under the bridge, he thought putting down his drink. He picked up the phone and called the airport for a flight west. If he hurried, he could get out right away and be there by tonight. Let Sandra come home to an empty house and wonder where *he* was for a change.

Across town

FROM HIS HOT TUB on the master-bedroom deck, Bernard told George to send his guest up when she arrived. The water was hot, the jets relentless. He was sunk up to his neck, eyes closed. It wasn't long before he caught a whiff of her perfume. Opening his eyes, he found her framed in the doorway. He closed his eyes again, knowing when he opened them she would be waiting in the bedroom.

He took his time. He liked to make her wait. He dried himself and, breathing in her scent, moved through the large master bedroom, expectation arousing every nerve fiber.

She lay on her back across the end of his king-sized bed, buck naked, her eyes closed. He watched her chest rise and fall, her nipples already hard nubs. Her legs were long and shapely, her body as close to perfect as money could buy.

He let the towel wrapped around his waist drop to the floor.

She turned her head to look at him, watching him with a mixture of excitement and fear in her expression. He liked that about her.

He picked up the belt from where he'd left it on the chair near the end of the bed and looked down at her, their eyes locking.

Then slowly, he raised the thick leather belt, saw her tense, her eyes widening but never leaving his.

He brought the leather down sharply across her thighs. She let out a cry, arching her back. He lay the leather across her belly, her breasts. He had never wanted to hurt her as badly as he did tonight.

She didn't stop him, just as he knew she wouldn't. This is what she came here for.

To the sound of her soft whimpers, he finally tossed the belt aside. She was watching him again, almost daring him to do whatever he wanted with her.

"Tell me Jasmine is dead," she whispered as he rolled her over.

"Jasmine is dead."

Chapter Five

Antelope Flats, Montana

Molly was sick of sagebrush. She'd been driving on two-lane blacktop highways for what seemed like days, passing through tiny dying towns and miles and miles of barren landscapes.

Not far inside the Montana state line, she saw what appeared to be a small cluster of buildings on the horizon. A mirage in the middle of nowhere. A few miles up the road, she spotted the city limits sign: Antelope Flats.

She couldn't believe her eyes. She'd expected small, but this town was even smaller and more isolated than she'd imagined. She'd expected it would be backwoodsy, but not to this extent. The western town seemed trapped in another time, the buildings straight out of an Old West movie.

She drove through town. It didn't take long. Then she turned around, stopping to shake her head and laugh. Well, she'd wanted to disappear in a place where Vince and Angel would never think to look for her. And it appeared she'd gotten her wish.

Getting into her role, Molly had put on at least five pounds, changed her makeup, lightened her hair and bought herself some conservative clothing, something she thought a woman like Jasmine Wolfe might have worn. Coming from the South and a wealthy Atlanta family, Jasmine had to have a whole lot of conservative in her background.

Molly had watched the newspapers as she worked her way toward Antelope Flats. Jasmine Wolfe's body hadn't been found as of yesterday. Nor had the woman turned up.

As Molly drove back into town, she couldn't help but wonder why a woman with Jasmine Wolfe's money and background would want to live here, let alone marry the sheriff.

The town seemed even smaller this time around. If she had blinked, she would have missed it. She pulled up in front of the small brick building on the edge of town with the sign Sheriff out front. It was late and she'd worried that she might not catch him before he left for the day.

But as she turned off her car engine, she noticed a car marked Sheriff was parked in front. No other cars were on the street except for a few muddy pickups at the other end of town outside the Longhorn Café.

She glanced toward the front window of the sheriff's office but the slanting sun was shining on the glass, making it more like a mirror. She took a breath and reminded herself that she was the daughter of Maximilian Burke. Even rusty from lack of sleight-of-hand practice, she could do this.

But she didn't kid herself, she would have to give the performance of her life to pull this off. If she blew it, she had a lot worse to worry about than attempted fraud charges.

Taking her purse and the first newspaper article and photo, she got out of the car and walked to the door of the sheriff's department. Tentatively she tried the door. Unlocked. She pushed the door open, sliding a little too easily into the other woman's skin, a little too easily into that former life of lies, as she stepped inside.

By late afternoon Cash had made a half dozen calls as well as copying Jasmine's case file. He was surprised that he hadn't been relieved of his job yet. He knew it was only a matter of time.

Cash had covered his tracks as much as possible and was just finishing up when the phone rang. He picked it up, afraid it was going to be Investigator Mathews with bad news.

It was Jasmine's insurance company calling back.

"It took a while for me to find the policy," the agent told him. "This particular policy was canceled almost seven years ago due to the car being stolen?"

Something like that. "I need to know if an accident claim was filed. In September seven years ago? It would have been right after she bought the car." Cash listened to the shuffle of papers.

"None that I can see. September? Sorry. No claim."

He raked a hand through his hair, leaning back in his chair, letting go of the breath he'd been holding. So Jasmine hadn't filed a claim or reported the accident. He thanked the agent and hung up.

Now all he could do was wait. But he'd been waiting for either a call that Jasmine's body had been found or that he was being suspended until the investigation was completed.

But neither call had come. Everyone in the city offices next door had gone home for the day.

He got up from his desk, too anxious to sit any longer. He should go home. If Mathews caught him in his office… He moved to stand in the back doorway. Here he could catch the faint breeze in the pines out back. The spring evening was hotter than normal and his office had no air-conditioning. Hell, few places in Montana had air conditioning.

He didn't want to leave just yet. He was waiting for a call back from the Dew Drop Inn, a bar on the outskirts of Bozeman. He knew Mathews would eventually check on the matchbook found in Jasmine's car. Cash hoped to beat him to it. Mathews would be furious, but Cash would have to deal with that when it happened.

Right now, he needed answers, answers he should have gotten seven years ago. All these years he'd pretended Jasmine was alive. He couldn't pretend anymore. At any moment, Mathews would call to say her body had been found in a shallow grave on the farm, that she'd been murdered.

For years, he'd put his life on hold, unconsciously waiting for that call. Now, it seemed the wait might be over.

Behind him he heard his office door open. He turned. His heart seized in his chest, all breath gone, all reason evading him as he stared at the woman standing in the doorway.

"Jasmine." Her name was out before he could call it back.

She looked startled, as if she hadn't seen him standing at the back of the office.

His heart lodged in his throat, his senses telling him something his mind refused to accept now that her car had been found. Jasmine was *alive?*

"I…I…" She started to turn as if to leave and he finally found his feet, lunging forward to stop her, half-afraid she was nothing more than a puff of smoke that would scatter the moment he touched her.

She took a step back, seeming afraid, definitely startled. He stopped just feet from her, struggling to rein himself in, fighting to believe what was before his eyes. My God, could it really be her? Jasmine? Alive? He could only stare at her. How was this possible?

She stared back, her green eyes wide. "I was looking for Sheriff Cash McCall," she stammered, still angled as if she might bolt at any moment.

He cleared his throat, confused. "I'm Sheriff Cash McCall," he said, realizing with a start that there was no recognition in her expression.

"I'm…I'm—"

"Jasmine, Jasmine Wolfe," he said, the cop in him thinking of the blood found in her car, the seven years no one had seen her or the fact that she didn't seem to know him from Adam.

She shook her head and held up what appeared to be a newspaper clipping, the edges torn, the print smudged as if she'd spent a lot of time looking at it. "I'm not sure, but I saw this and I thought…"

He took the clipping she held out, glanced away from her just long enough to recognize the Associated Press story about the discovery of her car.

"The woman looked like me...." She stopped. "This was a mistake." She reached behind her for the doorknob.

"No." He hadn't meant to speak so sharply. "Please, don't go." He took a breath, tried to slow his racing pulse, tried to make sense of this. He'd been expecting a call that her body had been found, not this.

He stared at her, unable to take his eyes from her. Somehow Jasmine had survived. True, she looked different in ways he couldn't put his finger on. But one thing was perfectly clear, she was more beautiful than even in his memory.

But where had she been all these years? And why was she looking at him as if she'd never seen him before and was as shaken by what she saw?

He stared into her eyes. She'd didn't remember him.

Or maybe she did and was only pretending not to.

All he knew for sure was that if Jasmine had escaped the grave, then she would be back after only one thing. Vengeance.

MOLLY KNEW SHE WAS GAWKING but she couldn't help it. To say Sheriff Cash McCall was nothing like she'd imagined was a major understatement. And it wasn't just because he was drop-dead gorgeous. Which there was no denying he was. Tall, broad-shouldered, blond and blue-eyed but rugged looking. He wore western-cut jeans, boots and a short-sleeved, tan uniform shirt. A blue jean jacket hung over the back of his desk chair and close at hand was a pale gray cowboy hat.

It wasn't his looks that surprised her. It was the feeling that she'd been headed here her whole life. As if everything else had just been time spent waiting for this moment.

She met his gaze and quaked inside at the rush of feeling. There was some powerful chemistry here that drew her to him and at the same time, warned her to be careful. Very careful.

"Jasmine," he said again in his deep voice. "I can't believe this."

The sound of his voice seemed to echo in her chest, a drumming like that of her pulse. She tried to steady herself. *Calm down. This is working.* Just as she'd thought, she looked enough like the woman with the changes she'd made to fool even Jasmine's fiancé. As Max would have said of one of his magic tricks, "This definitely plays."

The talent required to perform magic or a con was showmanship. Only a small percentage of the act was the actual *trick*. It was amazing what could be done with a little misdirection.

She shook her head and backed away, using everything Max had taught her. "This was a mistake. I'm sorry."

He closed the distance between them, his fingers clamping over her wrist. He was strong but she cried out more in surprise than actual pain.

He quickly released her. "I didn't mean to hurt you. Please. Don't go."

She had him. So why did her instincts tell her to run?

The "tricks" with her father hadn't been this up-close-and-personal. She could see the combination of hope and naked relief in his eyes. He loved Jasmine.

Molly knew what it was like to lose someone she'd loved. Clearly, Sheriff Cash McCall had never gotten over that loss. She hadn't considered that after seven years he might still be in such pain. She didn't have to look to know that there was no wedding band on his left hand. She doubted there was even a woman in his life. But what guy would wait around for a woman seven years knowing she might be dead or just never coming back?

Sheriff Cash McCall obviously.

He seemed to be staring at her in a kind of bewildered amazement. "If there is any chance that you're Jasmine—"

"There isn't," she said.

"Please. Something made you come here."

Right. Two killers and the need for a place to hide.

"Please," he said again. "Sit down for a moment. What do you have to lose?"

She didn't even want to think about that. She must have been out of her mind. Her father's genes obviously coursed through her veins because she'd latched on to this idea without thinking it through. She hadn't expected to feel like this.

He smiled reassuringly and stepped back, giving her space. "Won't you sit down? Please."

There was a kindness in his voice, a calmness in his movements, although she could see how badly he needed her to be his fiancée.

All she had to do was *load* the hat—slip in the rabbit that she would later pull out as if by magic. She had him right where she wanted him. So why did she feel so miserable about it?

And even more alarming, why did she feel like he had *her?*

Either way, she couldn't walk away now. She was in too deep. She had no choice but to stay and play this through. She couldn't admit that she'd known all along she wasn't the missing woman, whereas if she stayed, he would realize eventually she wasn't his lost love. He would be hurt. She would feign disappointment, sorry that she'd gotten his hopes up. No harm would have been done.

Right, you just keep telling yourself that.

She gave him a tentative smile and took the chair he offered her. He pulled up one next to her rather than go behind the desk. She could see that he didn't know what to do with his hands. They were large, the fingers long and finely sculpted, tanned from the sun, callused from some type of manual labor and definitely strong.

She shifted her gaze to his eyes, the same pale blue as summer skies. There was something so appealing about Cash McCall….

"Why do you think you're not Jasmine?" he asked quietly.

That one was easy. But she could hear Max saying, "Don't be a fool. Have you forgotten Vince and Angel and what they'll do to you if they catch you? Stall for time. You're safe here. And there just might be a pot of gold at the end of the rainbow, kiddo."

She felt sick and realized she was more like Max than

she'd ever admitted. She had only thought of herself. And now she was in trouble. So like Max.

"I know I look like her, but I can't see how…" She made a motion with her hand, swallowed and looked around the office. It was sparsely furnished. A gold-framed photograph on his desk caught her eye.

"Your family?" she asked, indicating the photo of a group of blond, blue-eyed people standing at a wide porch railing.

"Shelby insisted on a family portrait," he said, looking uncomfortable. "She also insisted I put it on my desk. Shelby's my mother. She's a bit…bossy at the moment, probably always has been." He shook his head before she could ask what that meant. "It's a long story." He leaned forward a little, obviously trying to relax. Or at least make her think he was relaxed. "Tell me about *you.*"

Going in, she knew she couldn't lie about her name or her past—at least the past seven years of it because he was bound to check. There was no reason to anyway, since those years had been innocuous enough and her pattern of living would suggest that she'd been unsettled, lost, searching for something.

"For as long as I can remember, I've traveled from one place to another," she said honestly. "My name is Molly Kilpatrick. At least that's what I've been going by." She'd learned at an early age that it was always best to blend as much truth as you could with the lies. It made keeping the lies straight that much easier. You just had to be careful that you didn't start believing your own lies.

Meanwhile, she needed to make it clear that as far as

she knew, she was Molly Kilpatrick and any confusion on her part as far as her resemblance to Jasmine Wolfe was innocent. Even if he found out that she was the daughter of Maximilian Burke, she figured her father's death could easily explain her alleged lapses of memory.

"I've always had the feeling that something happened in my past, something traumatic that I want to forget, and that's why I can't remember," she continued. She described her life pretty accurately, at least the years since her father died.

When she finished, she saw that the sheriff was studying her intently. Magicians called it "the burn" when someone is watching you with an unblinking stare, looking behind your words and sleight of hand to see the "trick."

Cash felt like pinching himself. Jasmine. He couldn't have been more shocked or relieved. While she was saying she didn't believe she was Jasmine, he was looking at her face, the color of her hair, the sound of her voice, her mannerisms. All Jasmine. Only just different enough to account for the fact that she'd been lost for seven years.

"This is amazing," he said when she stopped talking. The cop in him told him he should be paying more attention to her story, but the man in him could only stare in wonder. Somehow Jasmine had survived—and found her way back.

To him, he realized with a start.

He would have expected her to contact her family. Or her old roommates. Except Sandra Perkins was married to Kerrington Landow now and who knew where Patty Franklin was.

He just found it hard to believe that she could come to him. Not after the last time he'd seen her. But maybe she really couldn't remember what had happened between them any more than she could remember him.

He tried to concentrate on what she was saying as she told her story haltingly, stopping occasionally to lick her lips. He tried to remember that mouth. It had been so long. Would it be the same if he kissed it?

When he'd thought of Jasmine over the years, the memories had been sharp and painful. Now though, as he studied her, he realized he'd forgotten how he'd felt, that initial first attraction, or how she'd tasted when he'd kissed her.

She stopped talking, then added, "That's why when I saw the article about Jasmine Wolfe…" Her eyes met his.

He remembered that pale green color. Only he'd remembered it as reminding him of cool jade, not warm tropical waters as it did now.

"You're not sure how many years you've lost?" he asked, trying to pay more attention.

She shook her head, catching her lower lip in her teeth. It was something he couldn't remember Jasmine ever doing.

"When I read that there was a search going on for her, I thought that if there was even a chance that I was…" She stopped, licked her lips again. "I didn't want people to keep looking for her if… I didn't want her family to…" She shook her head. "You must think I'm a fool to come here."

Jasmine had *never* been a fool. Nor could he imagine her thinking herself one. "No, you're no fool," he said studying her. "Can you remember anything about the day you disappeared?"

She shook her head slowly and let out a small laugh. "I didn't even know I'd...disappeared."

He smiled realizing that, from her perspective, that was probably true. "Have you seen a doctor about your memory loss?"

She nodded. "He said sometimes a blow to the head can cause it. I would imagine that's where I got this." She lifted a lock of her blond hair away from the left side of her forehead.

The scar was shaped like a crescent moon, pale white and about an inch and a half long. He drew in a breath and let it out slowly. Head wounds bled a lot. That would explain all the blood in her car.

He felt a wave of relief. Not that she didn't look and act like Jasmine, but the cop in him had questioned how she could be alive given the large amount of blood that had been found in her car. The blood loss, the head injury, couldn't those both contribute to memory loss? And couldn't that explain why she'd just *disappeared* for seven years?

"You don't know how you got the scar?" he asked.

She shook her head. "It was just there one day when I looked in the mirror."

He could see that the scar had scared her. He tried to imagine just looking in the mirror one day and seeing a scar and not knowing when or where you'd gotten it.

It should have scared her, he thought. It certainly did him, just trying to imagine how she'd gotten it.

She absently touched the scar with her fingers. "I think I came here hoping to find…myself." Her voice broke a little and tears glistened in her eyes.

He'd never seen Jasmine vulnerable before. That he did remember. It took everything in him not to pull her into his arms. But he was a stranger to her. And she was clearly scared. The last thing he wanted her to do was bolt.

"I realized when I saw the photograph that I've put my life on hold for years waiting for something I didn't understand." She frowned. "Does that make any sense to you?"

He wished it didn't. He'd done the same thing and hadn't consciously realized he was doing it. With a start, he remembered that Bernard would be flying in. "Your brother—stepbrother—Bernard is on his way here. If he's not already here."

Her eyes widened in alarm. She shook her head. "But what if I'm not Jasmine? I don't want to get his hopes up."

Cash doubted Bernard's hopes would be raised by the thought of Jasmine being alive. Bernard had inherited everything when Archie had died, as far as Cash knew. And knowing even as little as he did of Bernard, Cash couldn't see Bernard wanting to share it with a stepsister back from the dead.

"It would be like him losing his sister all over again," she was saying. "And I couldn't bear to think I had a brother only to have him snatched away if I'm right and I'm not Jasmine."

Losing Bernard wouldn't break anyone's heart, Cash thought. "You don't have to see him if you'd rather not."

Her relief was almost palpable. "It's not that I don't want to see him. Later. If I really am Jasmine. Isn't there some way we can keep this quiet until we know for sure?"

He hated to tell her how impossible that would be in a town the size of Antelope Flats. He had to tell State Investigator John Mathews. But he had no way of reaching him at this hour. Cash couldn't see what it would hurt to wait. Mathews would do everything he could to keep the story from blowing wide open, but he would want to question Jasmine—and in her state, Cash feared she would take off again.

Cash knew he was just making excuses.

What he needed was time. Before anyone else got involved, he had to be sure in his own mind that she really was the woman he'd spent seven years trying to forget.

"Maybe there is a way to keep it quiet," he said, watching for her reaction. "I can take your fingerprints and send them to the FBI. They have Jasmine's on file."

"How long will it take to get the results?" she asked without even a blink.

He would send them to his friend in the FBI. With luck he would know by tonight, but he didn't tell her that. "It usually takes a week. Maybe more."

She seemed relieved rather than upset by that news. He got the feeling that things were happening too fast for her.

"I'll just stay in a motel out of sight until then."

"Your brother will be staying at the only motel in town."

She looked surprised, then worried. "What can we do?"

We? A sliver of doubt embedded itself under his skin.

He told himself he was just being a cop. She had come to him, she needed his help. Of course, she would say "we." So why was he suddenly suspicious of her motives?

Because she'd involved him so slickly into a conspiracy to keep her existence a secret. It worked perfectly into his plan to have her to himself until he could decide if she was really Jasmine—and what she wanted.

But he had to wonder if it also worked perfectly into some plan she had.

"If anyone finds out that I came to you before we know for certain if I'm Jasmine… Can you imagine what would happen if the newspapers got hold of this story?"

He could well imagine. His life had been blown wide open for months after she'd disappeared. But she didn't need to sell him any further on hiding her. "There might be a way to keep you hidden until we have proof that you're Jasmine." He let the words hang in the air for a few moments, not wanting to act too eager. "You can stay with me."

Her surprise almost seemed genuine. "Oh, I couldn't."

"I have a large house. There is plenty of room. It is the only way to stay hidden in a town this size. Unless you'd rather not, under the circumstances."

She frowned. "Circumstances?"

"The general assumption was that you were abducted by a man at the gas station who is now in prison," Cash said. "But for several reasons I don't think that was the case."

"What reasons?" she asked, sounding more curious than worried.

"First off, the man serving time in prison right now was offered a deal if he told them what he'd done with you. He didn't take the deal. I don't think he was the one the station clerk saw get into your car." He was watching her, not exactly sure what he was looking for, just a feeling that he should be leery of her. Especially if she was Jasmine.

"Secondly," he continued when her expression didn't change. "You would never have gotten into your car with a stranger even if he was holding a gun on you. You'd been taught what to do because kidnapping was a real threat given your family's wealth. The only reason you would leave with the man at the station was because you weren't afraid of him."

That last seemed to finally get a reaction out of her. "You think I *knew* the man who abducted me?"

He nodded slowly. "A man who left you for dead seven years ago."

"You're telling me that if I'm Jasmine Wolfe, I'm lucky to be alive."

"Oh, I think you got *very* lucky. The problem is, if I'm right, your assailant won't be happy to hear you're alive and can identify him."

"But I can't! I don't remember anything about that day."

"My point exactly. You could be in the room with a killer and not even know it. Until it was too late."

She bit her lower lip as if considering that she might be in danger. "I guess the safest place I could be now is with the town sheriff," she said with a nervous laugh. "Right?"

He cleared his throat and met her eyes. "Right." Unless, of course, she was going home with the prime suspect in Jasmine's disappearance and attempted murder.

Chapter Six

Molly couldn't believe how easy it had been as she watched Cash prepare to take her fingerprints.

She'd come away *clean* without getting caught with any cards up her sleeves. As Max used to say when he'd fooled someone in the front row of the audience with one of his magic tricks, "I could have gone south with an elephant in front of that guy!"

Not only did the sheriff buy her as Jasmine, he'd also agreed to keep the news quiet—and was taking her home to his house. She couldn't have asked for a better place to hide out.

There had only been that one surprise. Cash seemed to think Jasmine had known her attacker, that the person was still at large, that her attacker had left her for dead. And now with Jasmine back, Molly's life was in danger.

It was her karma and the risk that went with stealing a dead woman's identity, she thought bitterly. Wasn't it bad enough that she already had two killers after her?

She hoped that Cash was just being cautious. He

seemed a cautious man. Of course he could also just be trying to scare her. If he knew she wasn't Jasmine, what better way than to make her think she was in danger from a killer if she continued this charade.

No, she thought, studying him. He believed she was Jasmine because he wanted to. Maybe he really was worried about her safety. Maybe the man now in prison for abducting those other women really hadn't picked up Jasmine at that filling station.

Good thing she wasn't planning to stay in this gig long. And there was always the chance that Cash was wrong. The cases were too similar not to have been the same man—even if the man now in prison hadn't confessed to Jasmine Wolfe's abduction.

"Yes?" Cash said. He was looking at her, studying her again as if he saw her struggling with her thoughts.

She shook her head. "Nothing. This must come as a shock to you." Her prints weren't on file anywhere. That was one reason she hadn't been able to get a job at a Vegas casino. Casinos took all employees' fingerprints as a matter of course. But still, she felt a little anxious to think he was about to send them to the FBI. Did that mean they would be on file from now on? Good thing she was going straight again after this.

He reached for her hand. His fingers were warm and she felt a small thrill ripple over her as he began to take her fingerprints. She mentally kicked herself as he raised a brow at her reaction. Cash McCall didn't miss much.

"Am I anything like her?" she asked grabbing hold

of every magician's best defense—misdirection and patter. Talk about anything. Just draw the audience away from what you're really doing. "I mean other than the way I look?"

He took her fingerprints, carefully getting a perfect print from each finger. He didn't look at her as he worked. "You sound like her and some of your mannerisms remind me of her," he said after a few moments.

"Were we close?" she asked shyly.

His gaze came up to meet hers. There was heat in it and although it had been a while, she recognized the look for what it was: desire.

"We were engaged, weren't we?" He looked back down.

"I know this must be hard on you," she said, "I'm sorry I don't remember...us."

He finished taking the rest of her prints before he looked up again. "Here, you can clean the ink off with this," he said, handing her a towelette.

"Thank you." She scrubbed at the ink, still watching him out of the corner of her eye. When she'd asked about their relationship, he'd grown quiet, almost pensive. There was something he didn't want to tell her.

"I'll send these in," he said, getting up, turning his back to her.

"I'm sorry."

"What do you have to be sorry about?" he asked over his shoulder as if surprised.

"All these questions. But I don't know much about Jasmine. Just what I've read in the papers...." She pretended to hesitate. "And there are so many questions that only you can answer."

He took a breath and let it out slowly as he finished taking care of the prints. "What do you want to know?"

She shrugged. "Anything you can tell me. How did you meet?"

He took his chair behind his desk, giving her his full attention. "I was teaching a class in criminology at Montana State University in Bozeman. We ran into each other in the hall." He shrugged. "The next day you were waiting for me outside my classroom."

Jasmine hadn't been a shrinking violet, had she?

"How long did we…you date?"

"Not long. The engagement was kind of…sudden." He smiled a little as if embarrassed and met her eyes. "I'd never met anyone like…you."

And she'd thought he was a cautious man. Probably was. Except when it came to women. Or at least one woman. She felt a prick of jealousy and wondered what kind of lover he'd been. And Jasmine?

Cash was smiling. "You had another question?"

She really had to watch herself. He seemed to be reading every expression. "I was wondering about…our relationship, that is, yours and Jasmine's."

He laughed. It was a wonderful sound. "You want to know if we were…*intimate?*"

The word was so old-fashioned. Like Cash. She suspected he followed some Code of the West. "It's just if I'm going to stay with you…" She wasn't really blushing, was she?

"Are you worried about your virtue?" he asked.

There was an edge to his voice that surprised her. Had her question upset him because it was so personal? Or was it something to do with Jasmine?

"I know it's none of my business," she said quickly. "I shouldn't have—"

"We never slept together."

She tried not to look surprised by that—or the flash of anger she'd seen in his expression. Obviously their not sleeping together hadn't been his idea.

"Oh" was all she could think to say. She was no authority on relationships, since she never stayed long enough in one place to have anything long-term. And her idea of a short-term relationship was a dinner or a movie date. At almost thirty, she had never even been in love.

But any woman who wouldn't want to go to bed with Cash McCall needed her head examined. Her gaze fell on his hands, and desire stirred within at just the thought of those hands on bare skin.

"Her loss," she added ruefully and then could have bit her tongue.

He cocked his head at her as if taken aback by her comment. Not half as much as she was. The idea was to distract the audience during a trick—not shoot yourself in the foot.

An awkward silence fell between them, which she didn't dare try to fill. Who knew what she'd say?

"We should see about getting you to the house. I thought you could drive your car and follow me. It's only two blocks. We can put your car in my garage."

She glanced toward the open back door of the office. She could smell the sweet scent of pine coming from the growing darkness. "You're sure it won't be an imposition?"

"Having second thoughts?" He smiled but this time it didn't reach his eyes.

He's angry at Jasmine and he thinks I'm her. "Are you sure you're all right with this?" She wasn't sure she was.

His gaze flickered as if he hadn't expected any concern from her—and it touched him. "Don't worry about me. I can't promise that I can keep you a secret for long. But I will try until we get the fingerprint results."

"Would you mind calling me Molly?"

He nodded slowly.

"It's just that…"

"You don't have to explain," he said. "You're still not comfortable with the idea of being Jasmine."

She nodded. And it wasn't something she intended to get comfortable with. All she'd done was buy herself a little time. "Thank you. For everything. I appreciate you letting me stay at your house."

"Have you had dinner yet?"

She shook her head.

"I haven't been to the grocery store but I do have some leftover pot roast with vegetables from my garden."

She laughed. The man had a garden and he cooked. Unbelievable. "I *love* pot roast," she said, relaxing a little. There was nothing to worry about. He didn't suspect anything. She had to quit questioning her luck. Obviously, it had changed for the better.

But when she looked at him, he was frowning. "What is it?" she asked, realizing that she'd done something wrong.

He shook his head, quickly replacing the frown with a smile as if she'd caught him. "Nothing. It's just your…laugh. I'd forgotten…how much I've missed it."

She felt her stomach churn, but she forced herself to smile. Fear reverberated through her.

He had just lied to her.

And a few moments ago she would have bet anything that he wasn't the lying type.

Maybe she was wrong about him. Maybe she hadn't fooled him. With a shudder, she realized that she'd talked her way into staying at his house, alone with him, her car hidden in his garage. And he was the only person in town who even knew she existed.

Suddenly, that nagging feeling—that she would regret this—was back again, stronger than ever.

"Ready?" he asked from the doorway.

She started toward the door.

"Just follow me," he said. "It's the last house at the edge of town."

Of course it was.

"You can't get lost," he added.

She'd been lost her whole life. Right now she just wanted to run. Running was easy, she realized. That was probably why Max had been so good at it.

Cash looked at her as if he sensed her thoughts and had no intention of letting her out of his sight. "Don't worry. We'll figure this out together."

She walked to her car, unlocked it and climbed in. There were a few more pickups parked down Main Street in front of the Longhorn Café but other than that, the town was dead. As she inserted the key and started her car, he got into the patrol car. If she took off, he would come after her. Now how stupid would that be on her part?

He backed up and she followed him the two blocks to where he parked the patrol car in front of a large old house surrounded on three sides by huge pine trees. The house was at the edge of town, just as he'd said, no other house close by.

She pulled into the driveway in front of the separate garage and looked up at the monstrous place in the fading light. She'd never liked old houses. They were cold and rambling, smelling of age, often haunted with the lives of those who had lived there before, those hard lives worn into the steps, carved like scars into the walls, their lives still echoing in the high-ceilinged rooms.

She sat in her car and watched him get out of his and open the garage door. Now or never. She started to reach for the key when he appeared at her side window and motioned her to pull into the now open garage. She hesitated, but only a moment and drove inside. She turned off the engine, she pulled the key out and opened her door.

He smiled as if to reassure her.

She tried to smile, but realized she was ridiculously nervous. Max must be rolling over in his grave. She'd played it just right. She'd gotten what she wanted. What she needed. But if she didn't get control of herself she would blow it.

"What do you think of the house?" Cash asked. "I bought it for you as an engagement present. It was a surprise. Unfortunately, you never got to see it."

She didn't know what to say. He bought a rich woman an old house?

He was studying her, expecting a reaction. She could only nod at him and blink as if fighting tears.

He got her suitcase from the back seat and led the way up the steps. She braced herself as he opened the door and stepped aside for her to enter.

"THIS IS IT," CASH SAID as he reached in and turned on a light. Over the years, he'd thought about remodeling the house. He'd thought more about selling it. The house stood as a constant reminder of Jasmine and he guessed that's why he'd kept it. He never wanted to forget.

In the end, he'd done nothing. He'd been locked in a holding pattern, unable to move on with his life, unable to decide what to do with the white elephant, no desire anymore to fix it up.

He watched her come through the door wavering between his conviction that she was Jasmine and a nagging feeling that things weren't as they seemed. What had really brought her here? Not him. He was almost certain she'd come for something else. Whatever it was, he was determined to find out.

He was no fool. He'd seen the way she'd gotten him to invite her to stay here at the house. Well, she was here. Now what?

"It needs a little work," he said as he watched her take in the worn hardwood floors, the faded walls, the paint-chipped stair railing.

Her green eyes widened as she looked around. "It's...it's..."

He watched her struggling to find the words as he fought the urge to laugh. She hated it. He could see it on her face. She was horrified. Any doubts he had that she might not be Jasmine went out the window.

"I bought the house planning to restore it but I just haven't gotten around to it," he said. "I thought you, that is Jasmine and I would do it together."

"Oh? Well, it has all kinds of possibilities," she said, moving from the foyer to the bottom of the stairs.

"You think?" he said behind her.

"Definitely. It will be a lot of work but…" She turned and met his gaze, nodding. "Definite possibilities."

"I was hoping you would like it," he said and waited.

"Oh, I do. I'm sure Jasmine would have loved it, too."

He smiled at that.

"Buying her a house… Why, that's so…romantic," she said as if she needed to fill the silence.

"Romantic?" He couldn't help himself. He laughed.

She seemed surprised at first, as if not sure how to react, then she laughed with him. "I'm sorry, I just can't imagine anyone buying *me* a house."

He stopped laughing and looked at her. "I don't remember you being such a romantic."

"I'm sure I've changed," she said.

Boy howdy, he thought.

She looked so unsure of herself, he stepped to her, thinking only of comforting her, taking away that frightened, confused look in those green eyes. He cupped her face in his hands and felt the reassuring throb of her pulse, telling himself not to question this. Jasmine was alive—and he was off the hook.

She didn't pull away, her eyes locking with his and he felt himself diving into all that warm tropical sea-green. He leaned toward her, wanting to feel his mouth on hers, to taste her, to reassure himself.

But he caught a whiff of fragrance, something expensive and rare. The memory wasn't a pleasant one and not of Jasmine directly, but it was enough to make him jerk back, suddenly queasy.

She seemed surprised. Maybe a little disappointed. But also relieved? She straightened as if she had been leaning toward him as well. Now she looked away to brush invisible lint from the sleeve of her blouse as if embarrassed.

"I should show you to your room," he said, his voice sounding hoarse even to him as he picked up her suit-case and turned on the ancient chandelier overhead, throwing a little light on the stairs.

She was still standing in the foyer, looking as if she were shaken by what had almost happened moments before. He knew the feeling. Kissing her had been the last thing he'd planned to do and yet for a moment, he'd felt something so strong between them....

He shook his head at his own foolishness as he started toward the steps.

"Cash?" she said behind him.

It was the first time she'd said his name. The sound pulled at him like a noose around his neck, dragging him back to the first time he'd seen her. He stopped, one foot on the bottom stair, his heart pounding.

Slowly, he turned, not sure what he expected. The way she'd said his name, the sound so familiar, he thought she might say she'd suddenly remembered everything including the last time she saw him seven years ago.

That was why he wouldn't have been surprised to turn and see a weapon in her hand. He'd already seen murder in those green eyes.

But her hands were empty, her purse strap slung over one shoulder. She wasn't even looking at him, but staring through the doorway into the dark living room.

He followed her gaze, his eyes taking a moment to adjust with the shades drawn, and froze. Someone was sitting in his living room.

Las Vegas, Nevada

"I'M NOT GOING BACK to prison," Angel said as he cornered hard again.

Vince grabbed the door handle and held on. The car came down hard as Angel straightened it out and hit the gas, driving him back into the seat.

Horns blared, brakes screeched. Behind them, sirens wailed. Overhead, the dark shape of a police helicopter blocked the desert sun for a moment before Angel cut between two buildings, sending a crowd of pedestrians scattering, their screams dying off under the roar of the engine. Vince could almost hear the sound of a prison-cell door closing behind him.

"Did you hear me?" Angel yelled over the noise.

"I heard you. You'd rather die than go back to prison."

Angel jumped a curb, the car coming back down with another jarring slam. Vince closed his eyes. This was not the way he'd hoped his life would end. He thought of Max and how Max had made a run for it the day of the jewel heist. Foolish, very foolish. Going out in a blaze of glory. Only there was no glory; there was only blood and pain.

Not that Vince could convince Angel of that. He opened his eyes again as Angel cut through a casino parking lot, then another, then another until the sound of cop cars diminished just a little and there was no sign of the helicopter overhead.

Angel whipped into an underground parking garage and threw on the brakes. He was out of the car before it came to a complete stop. Vince got out too, his legs rubbery. He was getting too old for this.

He heard the shatter of glass, then the soft pop of a door opening. A moment later, an engine roared to life. Vince stumbled over to the vehicle, leaned against the side of it as Angel took off the license plates and switched them with another car in the lot.

Vince could hear the sirens growing closer. He thought about telling Angel to hurry, just for something to do, but Angel was good with his hands, quick, his movements efficient in ways his brain had never been.

The sirens grew louder and louder. He waited for Angel to get into the car and open the passenger side. All Vince wanted right now was to lie down in the back, close his eyes and trust that Angel would get them out of this—just as he had on numerous other occasions.

"You're going to have to get into the trunk," Angel said over the top of the car. He reached inside. Vince heard the soft click and whoosh as the trunk came open.

Angel was grinning, face flushed, eyes too bright. It

was that feeling again of standing under a power line to be even this close to him. Angel loved this. And that frightened Vince more than the sound of the approaching sirens.

"The trunk?" Vince said dumbly as he watched Angel knock the rest of the glass out of the side window and reach in the back for a cap that had been lying on the rear seat.

Angel put the cap on his head, adjusted it in the side mirror. "I would suggest you hurry."

All the other times Vince had just slid down in the front seat or hidden lying down on the back seat, but he could see that Angel was determined to have it his way this time—and there wasn't time to try to reason with him.

Vince moved to the gaping open trunk. The sirens were so close he could almost feel the handcuffs on his wrists. He climbed into the trunk, scrunched up to fit his large body into the cramped space. He hated tight spaces. And darkness. It reminded him of when his step-father used to lock him in the root cellar.

Angel slammed the trunk lid, the snap of the latch deafening in the pitch-black, musty darkness.

Chapter Seven

Molly heard again the soft rattle of ice in a glass, the same sound that had drawn her attention to the dark living room—and the man sitting there—in the first place.

She caught her breath as the faceless dark figure rose from the chair and moved toward her slowly, almost awkwardly.

Vince? He couldn't have found her. Not this quickly. Her pulse thundered in her ears. Run, her mind was screaming, but her feet seemed rooted to the floor.

As the man reached the light from the hallway, Molly saw with relief that he wasn't Vince. But the look on his face made her take a quick step back anyway. She heard Cash swear.

"Jasmine," the man whispered. "My God. You're alive." His face was ghastly white, his fingers holding the drink glass in his hand trembling, the ice in his drink rattling softly.

"What the hell are you doing here?" Cash demanded, stepping in front of Molly as if to protect her.

"The door was open," the man said vaguely as he peered around Cash to stare at her. He was soap-opera-star handsome dressed in chinos, a polo shirt and deck shoes. But next to Cash, he looked like a cardboard ad cut out from a fancy men's magazine.

"So you just made yourself at home?" Cash demanded.

The man was obviously shaken, deathly pale with beads of sweat breaking out on his upper lip. Molly thought he might be either drunk or dazed. Or both.

She wondered how he knew her. That is, Jasmine.

"Who the hell do you think you are?" Cash snapped.

Yes, Molly thought, who are you? And how did you know Jasmine? One thing was clear, Cash didn't like him. Nor did the man like Cash.

The man seemed to drag his gaze from her to look at the sheriff. "I needed to talk to you," he said, glancing down at the drink in his hand as if surprised to find it there. "I called the state investigator. He said I might find you here since you wouldn't be at your office. The door was unlocked so I helped myself to your Scotch."

Cash stood ramrod straight, his hands balled into fists at his side, anger in every line of his body. "We don't lock our doors in Antelope Flats," he said biting off each word. "Normally we don't have to. What do you want, Kerrington?"

"Kerrington?" Molly repeated in surprise, recognizing the name from one of the articles she'd read about Jasmine's disappearance.

"The *first* man you promised to marry," he said, scowling at her. "As if you don't remember."

"She *doesn't* remember," Cash snapped. "She's suffering from some kind of memory loss."

Kerrington stared at her. "Right," he said and let out an unpleasant laugh. As if playing along, he held out his hand. "Kerrington Landow." His hand was damp and cold from the glass he'd been holding, his grip too firm, as if he thought he could feel the truth in her pulse. "Still want to pretend you don't know me?"

"I'm afraid I don't know you," she said. "I'm sorry." But she wasn't. She didn't like the man.

He glared at her. From his expression, she couldn't tell if he was glad Jasmine might be alive or just the opposite.

Cash cleared his throat. "Now if you don't mind…" He grabbed for Kerrington's arm as if to show him out.

"I'm not leaving until you tell me what the hell is going on here," Kerrington said, drawing back out of his reach. "I thought the state investigators were still looking for her body out at that farm?"

"They are," Cash said. "She might not be Jasmine."

"So the state investigator doesn't know she's alive?" Kerrington said.

Molly decided the man was both drunk and dazed. And dangerous. She stepped in quickly. "Sheriff McCall, I don't want Mr. Landow going away with the wrong impression." She had to convince Kerrington that he couldn't believe his eyes before he blabbed this all over town. She was counting on being long gone before it hit the newspapers.

"I know I resemble Jasmine," she said reasonably.

Kerrington nodded and looked smug as if he were finally going to get the truth out of her.

"There is a lot about my past that I can't remember," she said. Or don't want to remember. "So I came here looking for answers. The sheriff has been kind enough to send my fingerprints to the FBI to be compared to Jasmine's. I'm staying here, out of sight, until we know for sure who I am."

"*You're* hiding her?" Kerrington said and shot a look at Cash, who groaned. "You think I don't know about the fight you had with Jasmine? And now her car turns up just a few miles from town…. I think the state investigator needs to know what you're up to."

"I'm not up to anything," Cash said between gritted teeth. "What are you doing in town, anyway? Jasmine isn't your concern. Or is she? I never bought your alibi, Landow."

Kerrington jerked his head back as if Cash had slugged him. "I didn't kill her. I have an alibi. And anyway she's alive, right?" He looked at Molly. "You're just trying to confuse me, aren't you. Make me say something you can use against me."

"I think we're all getting upset here for nothing," Molly said quickly. "Let's just wait for the fingerprint report to come back from the FBI. I don't believe I'm Jasmine Wolfe. My name is Molly."

"Molly," Kerrington said, nodding, but she could tell by his expression that he didn't believe her. "You look just like Jasmine. You sound just like her."

She wished now that she hadn't gotten Jasmine's voice and mannerisms down quite so well. She'd been able to copy Jasmine's faint southern accent flawlessly from the videotape. Jasmine's inflection, mannerisms and tone had been easy for someone who'd learned to mimic from the time she was a child.

"It would be a mistake to assume I was Jasmine, though," Molly said. "I don't want anyone looking like a fool because of me. If you were to tell people…" She saw Kerrington reconsider, just as she knew he would. She'd learned to read people. His worst fear would be to look like a fool.

"When will you get the results on the fingerprints?"

"At least a week, probably two," Cash said, sounding as if he hoped this didn't mean that Kerrington would stick around that long.

Molly could see Kerrington considering his options. "This isn't some kind of a trick?"

And to think Kerrington hadn't looked that perceptive, she thought darkly. "Why would I lie to you?"

He suddenly looked drunker, as if the Scotch he'd poured for himself was one of many he'd already had today. "That's what I'm trying to figure out." He looked at the drink in his hand again, must have thought better of finishing it and handed the half-full glass to Cash. "I should go."

"I agree," Cash said. "I hope you're walking, otherwise I'm going to have to drive you."

"I walked," Kerrington said straightening. "I'm staying at the motel. The only one in this damned town." He seemed about to say something but changed his mind as he looked at Molly for a long moment, then left without another word.

"He'd *better* be walking," Cash said, going to the door to look after him. Kerrington was. Otherwise Cash would have seen his car parked out front. Molly figured Cash probably knew what everyone in town drove.

He closed the door, locked it and turned to look at her. His jaw was clenched, his body still rigid with anger. "I can't believe that jackass."

She wanted to ask him why he disliked Kerrington as much as he obviously did. Was it just jealousy? Kerrington had been engaged to Jasmine first. But Cash didn't seem like the jealous type.

"He's going to tell, you know," Cash said.

"Do you think he'll go to the press?"

Cash shook his head. "He'll tell your brother though. Jasmine's adopted brother Bernard," he amended. "That means Bernard will have to see for himself whether or not you're Jasmine."

"Is that bad?" she had to ask.

Cash swore under his breath. "It's not good."

She smiled and saw some of the tension uncoil from his body. "You don't like Kerrington."

He shook his head. "Sorry."

"I'm the one who's sorry. There is no way I could have been engaged to that man."

Cash's smile was tight. "Apparently he never got over you."

"Over Jasmine," she said, wondering more and more about the woman who had two men she'd promised to marry and both hadn't let go even after seven years. She must have been *some* woman.

"He's married to Sandra Perkins." He seemed to hesitate, waiting for a reaction from her. "She was your—Jasmine's roommate. They got married just a few months after you disappeared. I'd heard she was pregnant. Must not have been. They have no children that I know of. Doesn't act like a married man, does he?"

Molly felt for Kerrington's wife. "You think she's here in town with him?"

Cash shook his head. "I doubt she even knows he's here. And what the hell is he doing here, anyway?"

Kerrington would tell Jasmine's stepbrother Bernard Wolfe. But would either of them chance going to the press before the fingerprint results came back?

She had no way of knowing. She still believed she could pull this off. Not that she had much choice. But she'd learned from Max long ago that a magician stayed with the trick—even when he realized the rabbit was no longer in the hat.

Las Vegas, Nevada

VINCE TRIED TO SLOW his breathing, afraid he would run out of air in the car trunk before Angel stopped and let him out.

The car moved at a snail's pace. He could hear other traffic. He was cramped and couldn't move, the darkness seeming to close in on him. He tried not to think about it or how much air he had left.

He thought instead about Molly and what he would do once they found her. He could understand her fear—especially if she'd heard what had happened to Lanny.

He could even understand her running. It was calling the cops that had him mystified. She obviously didn't understand the concept of honor among thieves and that disappointed him more than he wanted to admit.

He felt the car speed up and tried to relax. It wouldn't be long now before Angel pulled over and let him out. He took a breath of the hot musty air, feeling light-headed. He guessed they were on the interstate now, gauging the speed and the smoothness of the road. It was getting hotter in the trunk, closer, tighter.

He was sweating profusely now, the smell of fear filling the tight space. His muscles were starting to cramp, he was having trouble catching his breath and just the thought of being trapped in the trunk brought on a panic attack.

What if Angel had made him get in the trunk for another reason besides hiding him? What if he planned to take him out in the desert and kill him?

Unlike him, Angel had never held much store in the fact that they had some of the same blood coursing through their veins. Angel wasn't the sentimental type. Angel would have killed his own grandmother if there were something in it for him.

Vince stiffened as he felt the car decelerate. The tires left the smooth pavement for a bumpy road that jarred every bone in his body. Why didn't Angel stop and let him out? Where the hell was he taking him?

After an interminable amount of time, Angel finally stopped.

Vince held his breath and listened. He could hear the tick-tick-tick of the motor as it cooled. A car door opened and closed, no sense of urgency in the movements. The door opened again. Vince heard the scrape of the key in the trunk lock. That was strange. Why hadn't Angel just pulled the trunk lever before he got out of the car?

The trunk lid rose slowly.

Antelope Flats, Montana

CASH LED THE WAY up the stairs to the bedroom where Molly would be staying, cursing to himself.

Kerrington. He should have known the moment he caught that fragrance. The memory of Kerrington's cologne was now all tied up in his memories of Jasmine.

Cash knew he should call State Investigator Mathews and inform him about this latest possible development before Kerrington did. Still, he hesitated. He would know about the fingerprints by tomorrow at the latest. The call could wait until then.

And maybe he would get lucky and find out what she wanted, whomever this woman was whom he'd invited to stay in his house.

Her reaction to Kerrington had certainly surprised him—and Kerrington as well. Not just a complete lack of recognition on her part, but she didn't seem to like him. It could have been an act, he supposed. It could all be an act. But at least Cash wanted to believe her dislike for Kerrington was real.

He couldn't put his finger on what was bothering him about her. Part of him acknowledged that she was different from the Jasmine he remembered—the memory loss aside. He told himself that seven years and not knowing who she was would make her different. Not to mention whatever had happened to her before her car ended up in that barn.

As she'd said, she felt something horrible had happened to her. Any change he thought he saw in her could be directly related to that. And she had the scar to prove it.

Or she could be lying, just as Kerrington had accused her, the scar from some other accident. Cash hated that he and Kerrington might ever agree on anything, but there was something about Molly Kilpatrick, something that warned him to be wary whether she was Jasmine—or a complete stranger.

When had he become so suspicious? He knew the answer to that one as he turned to look back at her. She had stopped at the top of the stairs and appeared to be studying an old photograph of the ranch.

"Is this your family's ranch?" she asked.

The photograph was of the original homestead, the old hewn-log cabin, a herd of longhorns grazing in a meadow behind it.

"Yes." And no, he thought. But the photo was the essence of the ranch, how it had all begun. If she was curious about what his family ranch was now worth…well then that was something else.

"It's the Sundown Ranch. My great grandfather drove a herd of longhorns up from Texas to start it."

She nodded as if she didn't know what else to say and he saw that she seemed nervous.

"If you'd be more comfortable at the motel…"

She shook her head. "No, it's just…" She waved a hand through the air and looked into his eyes. Hers were a warm Caribbean sea-green in the hall light, as inviting as a kiss. He remembered almost kissing her earlier with no small regret. "You don't know me and yet you offered me a place to stay. I could be a total stranger."

"Could be." He smiled ruefully. For strictly personal, selfish reasons he wanted Jasmine to be alive. Didn't want her disappearance hanging over him the rest of his life. He wanted her to remember everything. No matter who it hurt, himself included.

"I might not be the man you think I am," he warned her.

She met his gaze. "Or me the woman you hope I am."

"I'm not worried," he said, knowing that wasn't entirely true. "Are you?"

Slowly she returned his smile and shook her head. "No. I know it's the safest place for me to be right now."

Or so she thought, he mused. "Your room is right down here."

He led her to the door of the master bedroom and opened it. It was a large, bright room. Fortunately, the house had come with some furniture. The high, white iron bed frame was one of the pieces.

When the house was built, the room was wallpapered in a tiny flower print of yellows, greens, blues and pinks. The print had faded some but was still intact. This room had always seemed too large, as if it demanded double occupancy. That's why he'd opted for a smaller bedroom down the hall. He kept this one made up for the times Dusty or one of his brothers stayed over.

"There's a large bath in here," he said, stepping past her to push open the door.

She let out a cry of delight at the sight of the huge claw-foot bathtub.

"I guess it was made special, that's why it's so large." Large enough for two, he thought ruefully.

"I love it," she said as if she could see herself sunk in the tub.

He had to smile. "So does my sister. She left an assortment of bubble bath. Help yourself."

"Thank you." Her gaze came back to him. Her smile was shy, uncertain, her mouth turning up a little higher on one side. He didn't remember Jasmine ever smiling like that, but he'd forgotten so much…. And some things he would never forget.

He tried to swallow the lump in his throat as he put down her suitcase. "If you need anything just let me know."

He hurried out of the bedroom, the large room suddenly feeling claustrophobic.

Who *had* he invited to stay with him?

"Come down when you're ready," he called back. "I'll just heat us up some dinner."

By this time tomorrow, he should know. Twenty-four hours. And every moment of it he would be looking for Jasmine in this woman. And waiting. Waiting to find out the real reason she had come to him.

Atlanta, Georgia

THE WOLFE COMPANY JET was winging its way across the Midwest when Bernard got the call.

He checked caller ID and felt his pulse jump. Stay calm. He'd recognized the name on the caller ID. Patty

Franklin, Jasmine's former roommate. Seemed she hadn't married. Or if she had, she'd kept her maiden name.

He took a breath, not wanting her to hear anything in his voice that might give him away. "Wolfe here."

"Bernard?" Patty sounded tentative. She always sounded tentative. Didn't take a brain surgeon to figure out why Jasmine had befriended *her*. Can you say *doormat?*

"Yes?" He pretended he didn't recognize her voice. Hell, it had been almost seven years since he'd heard from her. He wondered how she'd gotten his cell-phone number.

"It's Patty. Patty Franklin?" she said. "Your sister's former roommate?"

"Patty." He tried to make that one word say, "Why are you bothering me after all this time?"

"I'm sure you've heard about Jasmine's car being found," Patty said.

The story he'd found out had gone national. *Everyone* had heard. "Of course."

"I've been so upset. Is there any more news?"

No, and there is no more money to keep your mouth shut either. "No, I'm afraid not."

"Well, I didn't mean to bother you," she said. "I just wanted to see if there was anything I could do. I've never forgotten her. She really was one of a kind." He couldn't argue that. "I guess you're coming to Montana."

Patty just happened to still be in Montana? He waited for her to make her pitch for more money and said nothing. Force her to ask this time.

"I know how hard this must be for you," she said hesitantly. "I should let you go. I just wanted to say how sorry I am and how much I appreciated your kindness when we lost Jasmine."

"Thank you for calling, but I have to keep the line open in case there is any news," he said and disconnected, turning off his cell phone just in case she called back and wanted another fifty thousand in kindness.

And what was that about "when *we* lost Jasmine"? Patty hadn't meant anything to Jasmine and she sure as hell meant nothing to him. Why had she called?

He wondered if he'd made a mistake by not offering her more money. She'd never really *blackmailed* him. At least not outright. She'd just made a point of mentioning how she would never tell the police anything that might make him look guilty because she knew he couldn't hurt Jasmine. And the next thing he knew he was paying for her college education. Jasmine would have liked that, he'd told Patty and she'd cried and agreed. What a dummy he'd been.

HE SWORE NOW AND LOOKED at his watch. He couldn't wait to get to Montana and get this over with. He tried to forget Patty. He hadn't heard from her in seven years, so maybe her call had been just what she'd said it was.

Maybe by the time he got to Montana, Jasmine's body would have been found and he could finally put Jasmine to rest.

"Amen," he said, but Patty's phone call was still bothering him. He contemplated how far he'd go to get rid of her if she tried to extort him again. One thing was certain. He wasn't giving her another cent.

Antelope Flats, Montana

MOLLY WAITED UNTIL SHE HEARD Cash's footfalls die off down the stairs before she let herself relax. What a day this had been!

She'd bought herself a little time. She should have been relieved. But Jasmine's brother would be in town soon, if he wasn't already. Cash was convinced that Kerrington would tell Bernard. How would she avoid *that* bullet?

Knowing that Cash would try to protect her made her feel all the more guilty. That and seeing how much he wanted her to be Jasmine, how much he'd obviously loved the woman.

She looked around the room and tried to tell herself that she was safe and that was all that mattered. No way could Vince and Angel find her. But was that all she had to worry about? Could Cash be right about Jasmine's abductor being someone she knew, someone who wasn't going to be happy to see her alive?

She couldn't worry about that now. She'd just had two close calls. Running into Kerrington and an even closer call with Cash. She'd almost kissed him. Had wanted to kiss him. If he hadn't pulled back—

He was already suspicious. Kissing him would have been stupid. Something had happened back at his office, she'd done something wrong. She still didn't know what it was but she remembered the doubt she'd glimpsed in his face.

The only thing that had saved her was his desperation to believe she was Jasmine, she thought with a chill as she glanced around the room. He'd bought this house for Jasmine? And kept it for seven years untouched? Had he expected her to turn up one day just as Molly had done?

He hadn't moved on with his life, that much was clear. But why, she wondered. Because he'd loved Jasmine too much to let go? Or for some other reason?

She remembered what Kerrington had said about a fight between the two of them. And her car turning up just a few miles from town. Was he insinuating that Cash had something to do with Jasmine's disappearance?

She shook off the bad feeling that came with the thought. Cash had loved Jasmine. He wouldn't have hurt her.

And yet he was hiding something from her. She'd seen it in his face when she'd asked about their relationship.

She took a breath and let it out slowly. *Don't borrow trouble. You're safe. At least for a while. With luck, Vince and Angel have been arrested by now.* She still hadn't heard anything about Lanny Giliano. She would call tonight. Maybe somehow he'd gotten away.

This would be over soon and she would be gone. Like it or not, she would again be Molly Kilpatrick, daughter of the Great Maximilian Burke, magician extraordinaire and thief.

It would be a far cry from the daughter of Archibald Wolfe and the Wolfe furniture fortune. A far cry from being the woman Cash McCall had loved, she thought.

She looked around the master bedroom. If Jasmine really were alive, Cash would be sharing this room with her.

With a shudder, Molly hurried downstairs, feeling as if she'd just walked across the woman's grave.

Chapter Eight

Outside Las Vegas, Nevada

At first all Vince saw was darkness as the trunk lid swung upward, then a blinding light. He recoiled, drawing back into the tight space, covering his head with an arm, gasping for what he feared would be his last breath.

When something touched his shoulder, he cried out.

"What's wrong with you?" Angel demanded. "You get sunstroke or something in there?"

Vince peered out from under his arm. He'd expected to see a knife in Angel's hand. But all Angel held was a flashlight. "You blinded me."

Vince could see his brother frowning. "You need help out or what?"

Vince shook his head. He'd just spent fifteen years in prison with murderers and worse, but he'd never been as frightened as when that trunk lid had swung open. It made him sick that he could even think his half brother would kill him. What kind of man was he?

"My legs are asleep."

"Here, take my hand," Angel said. Awkwardly, Vince crawled out of the trunk with Angel's help.

"So?" Angel said as Vince stood and tried to get feeling back into his limbs. Just as he'd suspected, Angel had driven out to an isolated part of the desert. He could see lights in the distance on the interstate and hear the distant hum of the traffic. His chest ached, heart still pounding too hard. He sucked in the hot desert night air and tried to calm himself.

"I'm okay," he said as if trying to reassure himself.

"That's all you have to say?" Angel sounded disappointed, angry. "I got us out of Vegas with dozens of cops chasing us. You think that was easy back there?"

Vince shook his head. "You saved us. You're the best. Thanks."

Angel nodded. Clearly he'd hoped for more but Vince wasn't up to it right now.

"Yeah, well, don't forget it. You need me."

Vince put a hand on his brother's shoulder. "I do need you," he said, his voice breaking with emotion.

"You sure you're all right?" Angel asked again, eyeing him.

"Fine. Great. I'm great."

"Then let's get the hell out of here," Angel said, slamming the trunk.

Vince walked around to the passenger side and threw up in the sagebrush before climbing into the car.

"Where to?" his brother asked, sliding behind the wheel.

With still-trembling fingers, Vince took the laptop

from the back seat where Angel had put it. He booted up the program and waited for the GPS tracking device to tell him exactly where they could find Molly. It was time.

Antelope Flats, Montana

MOLLY SAID SHE *LOVED* POT ROAST, Cash thought as he put the leftover roast and vegetables in the microwave.

Was she just being polite? He didn't think so. She'd almost seemed impressed. He smiled at the memory. If she was Jasmine, she was definitely an improved version.

The Jasmine from seven years ago had been the pickiest eater he'd ever known. She ate like a bird, always worrying about her weight, but also very finicky about what she ate. She would have turned up her nose at pot roast. Her tastes ran more to expensive restaurant cuisine, takeout, anything that came in white boxes or fancy-shaped foil impressed *her*.

The doorbell rang. Cash swore. He wasn't up to seeing Jasmine's brother Bernard. Not now. And he didn't want to put Jasmine-Molly-whoever she was through another scene.

He moved to the door and looked through the peephole, already deciding that if it was Bernard, he wouldn't let him in.

It wasn't. It was Shelby, his mother. And she knew he was home and, therefore, wouldn't give up until he opened the door.

He swore under his breath and glanced up the stairs as she rang the bell again. Molly was still in her room.

Now if she would just stay there until he could get rid of his mother. He opened the door before she could ring the bell again. "Shelby."

"I know I should have called first," she said as she stepped past him and into the foyer. "I wanted to see how you were."

"I told you—"

"I know what you told me," she said, stopping in the center of the hallway to turn back to look at him. "I'm worried about you." She sniffed the air and smiled. "At least you're eating. But I hate the idea of you eating alone."

"I've been eating alone for years." He hadn't meant to say it so sharply. "I'm fine. Really." He needed to get rid of her before Jasmine came down.

She was eyeing him as if she didn't believe he was fine. "I'm so glad you're coming out for dinner tomorrow night."

He'd completely forgotten he'd agreed to that. What would he do with Jasmine? He couldn't leave her. "Listen, Shelby, about that—"

But his mother wasn't listening. She was staring at Jasmine's pale pink denim jacket. He'd hung it by the door when he'd brought in her suitcase.

"You have company?" she asked, sounding surprised.

At just that moment, Jasmine appeared at the top of the stairs. She stopped, almost stumbling as she saw that he wasn't alone.

"Jasmine?" Shelby whispered, grabbing hold of Cash's arm to steady herself, a look of horror on her face.

CASH STARED AT HIS MOTHER. Not only had Shelby recognized Jasmine, she also sounded stunned to see her and not the least bit pleased. What the hell?

"You know Jasmine?" he asked, a little stunned himself. He'd just assumed his mother hadn't known or cared what was happening in Antelope Flats during the time she'd been pretending to be dead. He'd thought she and Jasmine had that in common.

"We've never met, if that's what you mean," Shelby said. "I just…know about her."

He stared at his mother, amazed that she continued to surprise him. Clearly she knew a lot more about Jasmine—and his relationship with her—than he would have guessed. Possibly more than anyone else knew.

Jasmine cleared her throat and looked to him as if waiting for an introduction—or an explanation for this woman's obvious shock and thinly veiled animosity.

"Forgive my manners," he said and motioned her down the stairs. "This is Shelby, my mother."

Jasmine smiled warmly as she came down the stairs.

Shelby clutched his arm tighter. He could feel her trembling and frowned as he realized it could be from fear. Or rage. "You're even more beautiful than you were seven years ago."

His mother's words echoed in his head. She'd seen Jasmine seven years ago? Just how much did his mother know? He felt sick. Was it possible she knew his secret?

"I thought you were dead," Shelby said. "I mean, we all did."

"You do have that in common," Cash remarked, hating the anger and bitterness he heard in his voice but at the same time wanting to defend Jasmine. Or at least this version of her.

His mother shot him a reproachful look as she let go of his arm. "When were you going to tell us that Jasmine was alive?"

"I'm not Jasmine, I'm Molly." She looked to Cash as if for help. "That is, I don't think I'm Jasmine."

Cash sighed and said, "She's been going by the name Molly Kilpatrick." He filled her in, giving Shelby the short version of how she'd seen the article and the photo and had come here to find herself.

"We won't know for certain until the fingerprint results come back in a week or so," Cash finished. Except he planned to know a whole lot sooner than that.

Jasmine held out her hand. "In the meantime, please, call me Molly."

Shelby took Jasmine's hand in both of hers. "All right, Molly." She sounded as if she didn't believe for an instant that this woman was anyone but Jasmine Wolfe.

Cash watched his mother, seeing not the woman who'd been trying to ease her way back into their lives but one who, like the grizzly sow, was ready to fight to the death to protect her cub.

He wasn't sure what surprised him more. The fact that his mother had known about Jasmine or her apparent fear for him and need to protect him.

"We need to keep Molly a secret until the fingerprint results come back," Cash said. "If word got out, the press would have a field day." Asa had somehow managed to keep Shelby's return out of the papers, but hadn't been able to stop this part of the state from talking about it. The Longhorn Café had been abuzz for weeks.

"Trust me, I won't breathe a word," Shelby said, meeting his gaze. "And I think you know how good I am at keeping secrets."

"Oh yeah."

"You have to bring Jasmine to dinner tomorrow night," Shelby continued.

"Molly," Jasmine insisted.

"Yes, Molly," Shelby said, her smile anything but inviting. "You will come to dinner out at the ranch, won't you?"

It was clearly an order. "That would not be a good idea," Cash said. It was bad enough that his mother knew about her. He didn't need his whole family knowing. And then there was whatever was going on between his mother and Jasmine.

"Don't be ridiculous," Shelby was saying. "Of course you'll bring her. The ranch is the safest place for her. I will swear the family to secrecy."

Cash groaned. "Our family has enough secrets."

His mother shook her head as if he was wasting his time arguing with her. "You can't leave Jasmine here alone and you've already promised to come to dinner. It isn't as if you can keep her locked up in this house for weeks while you wait for the fingerprint results."

He realized she wasn't going to take no for an answer. Nor could he tell her in front of Jasmine that he had no intention of keeping her here for weeks. Just until he got the fingerprint results. Or until he knew on his own whom she really was.

And then what?

He'd cross that bridge when he came to it.

"Come out about six," Shelby said, then gave Jasmine a forced smile and said she was looking forward to seeing her at dinner, before turning back to him. "Walk me to my car, will you, dear?"

Shelby Ward McCall wasn't the type of woman who needed a man to walk her anywhere.

"Okay," he said and shot a look at Jasmine. "I'll be right back."

"Nice meeting you," Molly said.

"What was *that* about?" Cash asked Shelby the moment he closed the front door behind them.

"You're sure she's Jasmine?" his mother asked, an edge to her voice that took him aback.

"If I was sure, why would I send her fingerprints to the FBI?"

"Cash…" Shelby gripped his arm, an urgency in her voice. "Don't trust her."

He laughed. "If I didn't know better I'd think you were being one of those no-woman-is-good-enough-for-my-son mothers." Except that she had happily welcomed both Cassidy and Regina into the family when Rourke and J.T. had brought them home.

"If that woman in there is Jasmine, she's dangerous," Shelby said.

He felt himself go cold inside just as he had earlier. "Why would you say that? If you know something, Mother—"

She didn't seem to notice that he'd called her *Mother.* "Don't pretend with me. Whatever you once felt for that woman, don't turn your back on her until you find out what she wants."

"This might surprise you, but I know what I'm doing."

She let go of his arm and gave him a tentative smile, worry in her eyes. "I'm sorry. But she fooled you once before. She'll try again." With that, she walked to her car with the stride of a woman half her age.

Cash watched her go, filled with a sense of regret that he hadn't known her all those years when she'd been pretending to be dead. She was a tough old broad, he thought with a smile.

But how much did she know? He hated to think.

Molly felt a chill the moment the front door closed behind Cash and his mother. The woman hated her. Molly had seen it in Shelby McCall's expression, felt it in her handshake.

"What have you gotten yourself into?" she whispered as she folded her arms to rub her shoulders, trying to fight off the icy dread that filled her. Being Molly Kilpatrick hadn't been any picnic, but being Jasmine Wolfe was turning out to be even worse.

What kind of trouble had Jasmine gotten herself into at the end? Something that had gotten her killed, Molly was pretty sure of that. Apparently, Jasmine had her share of enemies. And possible lovers. Unless she hadn't slept with Kerrington either.

She glanced toward the front door, wondering what Cash's mother was telling him about her. Not her. Jasmine. Being Jasmine was becoming more of a pain than she ever could have imagined. And possibly more dangerous as well.

The front door opened and Cash came back in. He frowned. "Are you all right?"

"Fine. Just a little chilly." *Kind of like that reception I got from your mother.*

"Here." He took a fleece jacket from the coat rack by the door, instead of her denim jacket. "It might be a little big but it's warmer than yours. The house can be a bit drafty."

"Thanks." She pulled on the soft fleece. The jacket was huge on her. He took one sleeve. She watched him roll it up, could feel his gaze on her face as he did.

"Your mother seems nice," she said.

He stopped rolling the second sleeve to look at her. He must think she was a complete idiot not to notice his mother's negative reaction to her. But he said nothing and after a moment, he finished rolling up the sleeve. "There. Warmer?"

She nodded. "Were they close? Your mother and Jasmine?"

"I had no idea my mother even knew you. You have no memory of her?" he said.

Molly shook her head. He was referring to her as Jasmine again. Isn't that what she'd hoped originally? That he and everyone else would think she was Jasmine?

"Hungry?" he asked.

Her stomach rumbled as if in answer.

"Let's get you fed before anyone else shows up at the door," he said and led the way into the kitchen as if nothing were wrong.

But Molly could see the change in him since his

mother's visit. He seemed even more wary of her—if that were possible. What had his mother said to him?

Molly had hoped to gain his trust. But she realized there were some large key pieces of the Jasmine puzzle missing—just as if she really *did* have amnesia.

Why wouldn't he be suspicious of a woman who'd vanished into thin air and suddenly turned up on his doorstep, so to speak, seven years later?

But she knew it was more than that. There were undercurrents here that she didn't understand. Something to do with him and Jasmine. And his mother seemed to know about it.

Molly could feel Cash pulling away from her and the irony was he seemed to be doing it not because he suspected she wasn't Jasmine—but because he thought she *was*. "Are you sure I can't help with dinner?"

"Thanks but I've had it warming," he said and motioned her to a chair at the table as he took a large casserole dish from the microwave.

As he lifted the lid, she caught a whiff of dinner and everything but food was pushed from her mind. The casserole dish was filled with thick, juicy slices of pot roast surrounded by lightly braised carrots, potatoes and onions—and if that didn't smell heavenly enough, he also retrieved warm rolls from the oven and a plate of real butter from the fridge.

"Oh, that smells *so* wonderful." She breathed in the scents as if she hadn't eaten in days. It *had* been hours. At the moment, she didn't care if he knew what she was up to or not. She didn't care that everyone she'd met who'd known Jasmine besides Cash seemed to hate her.

And what had been going on with Cash and Jasmine was still to be determined.

The woman had been his fiancée. He'd put his life on hold since her disappearance. But there was more to the story. Much more, she suspected. She thought about what Kerrington had said and was reminded of that old adage: If you've never thought about murdering someone, you've never been in love.

Cash handed her a large serving spoon. "Dig in," he said, taking the chair across from her.

She did, ladling the rich gravy over several luscious slices of pot roast, lightly browned small red potatoes, slivers of golden carrots and whole baby onions.

"May I?" he asked as he buttered himself a roll and offered to do the same for her.

"Please." She took a bite of the pot roast and one of the small onions, closing her eyes as she let the amazing flavors fill her senses. So this was *home cooking*.

"You like it?" he asked.

She opened her eyes. "I *love* it."

He handed her the buttered roll and watched as she took a bite. She felt the melted butter dribble down her chin. She licked her lips, laughed again without thinking and reached for her napkin. Too late.

He leaned across the table and touched his napkin to the edge of her mouth, then her chin. Her eyes locked with his. Her breath caught in her throat.

Then he drew back, looking embarrassed.

She wiped her mouth with her napkin, shaken. It had felt as if he were seeing *her*—not Jasmine. And for that instant, he'd looked at her with…desire—as if he could feel the chemistry bubbling between them and was as surprised about it as she was.

She dropped her gaze to her plate. "You're a good cook." It was the only thing she could think to say.

"Thank you."

He took a bite of his own meal and she did the same. They ate for a few minutes in silence. And she soon lost herself again in the food. She couldn't remember a meal that had ever tasted so wonderful and told him so.

"I'm happy to see you enjoying it," he said smiling, but from his tone she knew she'd made another mistake, that he'd seen the card up her sleeve.

She should have been worried. But the meal was too good and she was too hungry.

"Tell me about Jasmine's brother Bernard," she said as she took the second buttered roll he offered her. Misdirection, a magician's best friend. "What is Bernard like?" she asked, pretty sure if Cash didn't like him, she wouldn't either.

"Spoiled, arrogant, superior." Cash looked up at her. "I'm sorry. I shouldn't have —"

"No, I appreciate your honesty," she said quickly.

Cash looked down at his plate, took a bite, chewed, swallowed, then said, "I suppose you should know. Your brother thinks I had something to do with your disappearance." His eyes locked with hers. "As a matter of fact, he thinks I killed you."

Chapter Nine

Antelope Flats, Montana

The moment Kerrington got back to his room at the Lariat Motel, he dialed Bernard's cell-phone number. Not that Bernard had given it to him. The two hadn't talked in years. They didn't even like each other anymore. Maybe they never had. He'd had to copy the number from his caller ID before he left Georgia.

"Jasmine is alive," he said after the beep to leave a message.

"You hear me? Jasmine is *alive*. Call me." He left his cell-phone number and disconected, wishing he'd called from the motel land line so he could have at least slammed down the receiver. He wanted to smash something. Jasmine was alive and staying with the sheriff. How in the hell? He couldn't imagine this being any worse.

On top of that, he was trapped in a motel room that was smaller than his bathroom in Atlanta. What was he going to do? Just sit around and wait for Jasmine to remember?

He wished Bernard would call him back. He was so

desperate to talk to someone that he'd even take Sandra. He'd never liked being alone. If Sandra were here, he would have made a joke about the antelope print hanging on the wall and possibly even gotten a smile out of her.

Not that he was in the mood to joke. Nor would Sandra have been thrilled about this motel or staying in Antelope Flats. And she would have hit the roof when she heard that Jasmine was alive. He counted his blessings that she was in Atlanta. Nothing could get Sandra out here. Not after growing up in the West.

It was Jasmine's fault that he'd ever even met Sandra, let alone married her. He'd only started dating Jasmine's roommate to make her jealous. Instead, he'd gotten Sandra pregnant and ruined everything with Jasmine.

He groaned at his own stupidity, opened his cell phone and dialed his home number. The phone rang and rang. Either Sandra wasn't there or she wasn't picking up. Maybe she hadn't returned home, didn't even know he'd left.

He swore as he snapped the phone shut. He had worse problems than Sandra, he thought, rubbing his neck. Jasmine had looked right at him and hadn't known him. Or at least pretended she hadn't.

The sheriff had said she couldn't remember anything. What if it wasn't an act? He knew amnesia was rare, but he supposed…

No, this was Jasmine. Wasn't it just like her to return from the dead and pretend she didn't know any of them, jerk their chains for a while and then go in for the kill?

He couldn't stay in this motel room waiting for

Bernard to call or he'd go crazy. What he wanted to do was go back to the sheriff's house and confront Jasmine without the cop being there, but he knew that wasn't going to happen.

Jasmine was no fool. She knew exactly what she was doing by staying with the sheriff—and worse, McCall believed her act. What a fool.

Kerrington grabbed up the motel-room key and slammed out of the room, got into the SUV he'd rented and started the engine, belatedly realizing he didn't have any idea where he was going. It wasn't like there was anything to do in this town. Billings was hours away. He was stuck here.

He remembered a bar on his way in. The Mello Dee. He drove to the edge of town, just outside the city limits, and pulled under the flashing neon. The place needed a good coat of paint among other things. A small hand-printed sign said it was under new ownership. He didn't care, just as long as it was open and it served strong mixed drinks.

As he got out, he noticed there were only two other cars in the lot. A country song twanged on the jukebox as he opened the door. A couple was playing pool at one end of the large open room. Several older guys were sitting at the far end of a long, scarred wooden bar.

Everyone turned to look at him as he took a stool at the opposite end of the bar from the old guys. The patrons lost interest in him quickly and went back to what they were doing. The bartender, a woman with a head of spiky dyed red hair, was bent over the sink washing glasses.

An Important Message from the Editors

Dear Reader,

If you'd enjoy reading romance novels with larger print that's easier on your eyes, let us send you TWO FREE HARLEQUIN INTRIGUE® NOVELS in our NEW LARGER-PRINT EDITION. These books are complete and unabridged, but the type is set about 25% bigger to make it easier to read. Look inside for an actual-size sample.

By the way, you'll also get a surprise gift with your two free books!

Pam Powers

Peel off Seal and Place Inside...

LARGER-PRINT
FREE BOOKS
EDITION

84

THE RIGHT WOMAN

she'd thought she was fine. It took Daniel'
words and Brooke's question to make her realiz
she was far from a full recovery.

She'd made a start with her sister's help and
she intended to go forward now. Sarah felt as if
she'd been living in a darkened room and someone had suddenly opened a door, letting in the
fresh air and sunshine. She could feel its warmth
slowly seeping into the coldest part of her. The
feeling was liberating. She realized it was only a
small step and she had a long way to go, but she
was ready to face life again with Serena and her
family behind her.

All too soon, they were saying goodbye and
Sarah experienced a moment of sadness for all
the years she and Serena had missed. But they
had each other now and that's what
She held

Like what you see?
Then send for TWO FREE
larger-print books!

PRINTED IN THE U.S.A.
Publisher acknowledges the copyright holder of the excerpt from this individual work as follows:
THE RIGHT WOMAN Copyright © 2004 by Linda Warren. All rights reserved.
® and TM are trademarks owned and used by the trademark owner and/or its licensee

The Harlequin Reader Service™ — Here's How It Works:

Accepting your 2 free Harlequin Intrigue® larger-print books and gift places you under no obligation to buy anything. You may keep the books and gift and return the shipping statement marked "cancel." If you do not cancel, about a month later we'll send you 6 additional Harlequin Intrigue larger-print books and bill you just $4.49 each in the U.S., or $5.24 each in Canada, plus 25¢ shipping & handling per book and applicable taxes if any.* That's the complete price and — compared to cover prices of $5.24 each in the U.S. and $6.24 each in Canada — it's quite a bargain! You may cancel at any time, but if you choose to continue, every month we'll send you 6 more books, which you may either purchase at the discount price or return to us and cancel your subscription.

*Terms and prices subject to change without notice. Sales tax applicable in N.Y. Canadian residents will be charged applicable provincial taxes and GST.

If offer card is missing write to: Harlequin Reader Service, 3010 Walden Ave., P.O. Box 1867, Buffalo, NY 14240-1867

BUSINESS REPLY MAIL
FIRST-CLASS MAIL   PERMIT NO. 717-003   BUFFALO, NY

POSTAGE WILL BE PAID BY ADDRESSEE

HARLEQUIN READER SERVICE
3010 WALDEN AVE
PO BOX 1867
BUFFALO NY 14240-9952

NO POSTAGE
NECESSARY
IF MAILED
IN THE
UNITED STATES

The moment the woman looked over at him, Kerrington realized he'd just made a horrible mistake.

CASH SAW FEAR FLICKER in her green eyes before Molly said, "Bernard thinks you were responsible for Jasmine disappearing? That's ridiculous." She said it with almost enough conviction that Cash believed she meant it. "You *loved* her. You wouldn't have hurt her. Anyway, if her brother knew you, he'd know you aren't that kind of man."

Cash had to smile. "Thanks for the vote of confidence. You almost sound as if you've known me longer than a few hours."

"I'm a pretty good judge of character," she said. "Anyway, you had no reason to hurt her."

He didn't correct her. Instead, he slid the pot roast closer to her. "Well, with you alive, I guess that proves I'm innocent at least of killing you. But it remains to be seen whether or not I had something to do with your disappearance. Too bad you can't remember that day."

She helped herself to seconds while he buttered her another roll and one for himself—and said nothing.

There was no way Jasmine would have eaten even a small plate of pot roast, let alone two, and there was no way she'd have even touched a roll dripping with butter. Jasmine had been off bread long before the low-carb craze.

He felt the prick of a memory, Jasmine making a scene at a café when served iceberg lettuce. He tried to swallow down the bad taste the memory left in his mouth. He'd forgotten how much he'd disliked eating with her because she always picked at her food and complained.

So how could this woman who looked so much like

Jasmine actually be her? He told himself that losing her identity, her money, possibly almost her life and being forced to live a hand-to-mouth existence could change a person. But Jasmine Wolfe?

He couldn't see her changing even if she were homeless and starving. He had a flash of Jasmine digging in a garbage can saying, "Iceberg lettuce? You have to be joking. I'd rather starve."

He studied the woman across the table from him. Was it possible that the Jasmine he'd known and this woman really were the same person?

Jasmine *had* been one hell of an actress, playing any role she thought would get her what she wanted. But she wasn't *this* good.

He watched her clean her plate as if she'd never tasted anything so good. Watching her eat with such relish, such passion, he started to think of her as Molly—the last thing he wanted to do. "Would you like a glass of milk?"

She seemed surprised, as if she'd been lost in the meal. She smiled and nodded. "That would be nice."

Jasmine wouldn't touch milk, he thought as he went into the kitchen to the fridge. He brought back a tall glass of whole milk—not even two percent—and watched her chug half of it then smile and lick her lips. "Thank you. That was delicious."

He nodded. If she was Jasmine, he liked the changes, he thought, then realized he'd thought *if.* What if she wasn't Jasmine? He wanted her to be Jasmine even more desperately than he had earlier. He wanted her to be alive. Needed her to be alive. And he would have gladly taken this Jasmine over the last one.

But more and more, he realized he found himself thinking of her as Molly. Either way, his instincts warned him that it would be a mistake to misjudge this woman, whomever she was, but especially if she was Jasmine, didn't really have amnesia at all and had come back for blood. His.

"I was thinking about what might jar your memory," he said.

She looked up, swallowed and waited, her green eyes wide with innocence and interest.

"The only thing I could come up with was your prized possession. You waited months for it, special ordered it loaded." He shook his head. "I know it cost a small fortune at the time. If you'd like to see it, I might be able to pull a few strings."

Her expression was priceless. "Jasmine's *car?*"

"Your car quite possibly," he said.

She swallowed again. Clearly the car was the last thing she wanted to see. She looked…scared. He felt a start. Was it possible she wasn't faking her amnesia and she was afraid to go out to that barn because a part of her remembered the horrible thing that had happened in the car the day she disappeared?

And if she wasn't Jasmine? Why would a total stranger be afraid to see Jasmine's car?

THE MUSIC BLARED in the Mello Dee as the bartender smiled at him and, drying her hands on her apron, moved down the bar toward him.

Kerrington watched her, wanting to run. Maybe if he just turned around and left—but it was too late.

"Hi." She put a cocktail napkin down in front of him and smiled. "I know you, don't I?" she said, cocking her head to one side as she studied him.

"No. I'll take a martini."

She arched a brow at him.

"Sorry. I've had a bitch of a day."

"Haven't we all." She wore flip-flops, blue jeans and a halter top, four inches of her midriff bare above the waist of her jeans. She wasn't bad looking, about his age and she beat the hell out of the alcohol-less motel room, except for the fact that he'd recognized her.

She put the drink on top of the cocktail napkin without spilling a drop. "I never forget a face. I just can't put my finger on where I know you from, but it will come to me. It always does." She held out her hand. "Name's Teresa Clark but everyone calls me T.C."

"Bob. Bob Jones." He lied but wasn't even sure why, since he didn't think she'd ever known his name. Just his face. Now if she would just go away so he could enjoy his drink and a little peace and quiet. With luck, Bernard would call and give him an excuse to leave without making her suspicious.

"Bob Jones," she repeated.

He picked up the drink and turned on the stool to watch the couple playing pool, hoping she'd take the hint and go away. The first sip burned all the way down.

The alcohol buzz he'd had going earlier was gone. He needed a drink and then he would get out of here. So what if she remembered who he was? But he knew the answer to that one.

"It's driving me crazy," she said behind him. "I've

been told I have three talents. I never forget a face, I'm great in bed and I make the best damned margaritas this side of Mexico. Do I know you from Seattle? I spent five years out there."

"Sorry, never been there," he said without turning around. He drained his drink and slid off the stool, turning to put the glass on the bar while he dug in his pocket for his wallet.

"Wait a minute!" T.C. cried. "I've got it. You used to come to the Dew Drop Inn outside of Bozeman with that snotty blonde." Jasmine. "And her uptight brother. Oh hell, she's the one I saw in the paper. The one whose car was found near here." Then her eyes narrowed and Kerrington knew what she'd remembered. The last time she'd seen him with Jasmine.

North of Las Vegas

"WELL? DOES THE STUPID THING work or not?" Angel demanded, looking over at the computer screen on Vince's lap.

"It works," Vince said, more relieved than he wanted to admit. If he'd lost Molly, he wasn't sure what Angel would have done. He was beginning to wonder if he had the stomach for this anymore.

"So where is she?" Angel snapped.

"She's in Montana."

Angel looked over at him. "What would she be doing in Montana?"

Vince shrugged. "Her car isn't moving."

"You sure she hasn't dumped the car?"

He wasn't sure of anything right now. "She's in Antelope Flats, Montana." Or at least her car was.

"So we're going to Montana."

So it would seem. Vince hoped he was right about Molly not finding the tracking device and ditching her car.

"We'll have to pick up another car," Angel said. "This one is too hot. I'm thinking a car lot. Might not be missed for a while. We'll have to borrow more plates, too."

Vince nodded. He left all of that to Angel. His job was to find Molly. And now that she'd set the cops on them, they wouldn't be safe anywhere. They had to find her fast, get the diamonds and get out of the country.

"Molly wouldn't have run unless she had something to hide," Angel said. "And she wouldn't have called the cops on us."

"She's scared," he said. He knew scared.

"Well, when we find her, she's mine."

Vince looked over at him, imagining what Angel had in mind. It made him sick to his stomach, but he tried not to show his disgust. Angel was on edge, all that nervous tension back in his movements as he drove north.

"Once we have the diamonds, we'll get out of the country." Vince could tell his brother wasn't listening. Angel had his head cocked to one side, hearing another voice, one that seemed to be getting stronger, a voice Vince now knew he wouldn't be able to override.

Antelope Flats

"YOU'VE CONFUSED ME with someone else," Kerrington told the bartender as he slapped money on the bar and turned to walk out.

"No way," she called after him. "I never forget a face."

The door closed behind him and he grabbed the wall to hold himself up. T.C. had recognized him, remembered that he'd been with Jasmine at the Dew Drop Inn. What else did she remember?

"Oh hell," he groaned. What was he going to do?

He hurried toward his rental SUV, wanting to get away from the bar in case she followed him outside.

She didn't seem like the type to just let it go. He couldn't believe how badly he'd handled that. He should have admitted the truth. No big deal. Instead he'd pretended he wasn't the guy.

What would she do now? Call the sheriff? He groaned at the thought.

His cell phone rang, making him jump. He fumbled it from his pocket and snapped it open as he climbed into the SUV. "Landow."

"What the hell kind of message did you just leave on my phone?" Bernard barked. "If this was supposed to be some kind of joke—"

"Jasmine's alive. I saw her less than an hour ago."

"Are you drunk?"

"Sober as a judge. She's staying with the sheriff." He could hear Bernard's breathing increase and knew he had his undivided attention *now*. "She calls herself Molly and is pretending she has amnesia, but believe me, it's Jasmine and I'm afraid she knows exactly what she's doing."

Silence.

"You still there?" He rolled down his window, needing air. He looked back at the Mello Dee, thinking of T.C. "That's not all. Remember that bartender at that out-of-the-way place we used to go to up by Bozeman? The Dew Drop Inn?"

"What?"

"That bar where we used to meet up with Jasmine," Kerrington said. "Remember the bartender who called herself T.C.? She had that line about she was only good at three things: never forgetting a face, great in bed—"

"And she made the best margaritas this side of Mexico," Bernard finished.

"She's working at a bar here in Antelope Flats."

Silence. Then, "What is it you think Jasmine's up to?"

"I don't know. Why are you taking this so calmly?"

"Because it can't be Jasmine," he said. "There's no way. And who the hell cares if a bartender from seven years ago is working in Antelope Flats."

"She recognized me and put me with Jasmine."

"I told you not to go up there," Bernard said. "You should have just let me handle it."

"Yeah? Like you did seven years ago?"

"What is that supposed to mean?" Bernard snapped.

"You're the one who came to me for an alibi."

"That's right, Kerrington. And I never asked you why you so readily lied to give me one."

Kerrington said nothing into the silence.

"Why, after seven years, would Jasmine show up now?" Bernard finally asked.

"She says she saw the story about her car being found, saw her resemblance in the photograph and had to find out who she was."

"What about all that blood the cops found in her car? When the sheriff called me, he said the cops were treating it as a homicide. I doubt they would do that if there was any chance—"

"I don't know, all right? You didn't see her. I did. It's Jasmine. The sheriff sent off her fingerprints. He's waiting for the results. He didn't even want me to tell you that I saw her."

"Who else have you told?" Bernard sounded strange.

"No one. Just you. Who the hell else would I tell?" He thought of Sandra. Is that who Bernard had meant?

Bernard covered the phone and said something Kerrington couldn't hear.

"There someone with you?" Kerrington asked.

"I was talking to my pilot as if it is any of your business," Bernard snapped. "Jasmine mention where she's been?"

"I just saw her for a few minutes before the sheriff threw me out."

"Where are you staying?"

"You know there's only one motel in town. The Lariat." He felt depressed and told himself Sandra wasn't with Bernard. He'd been stupid to think she'd been with him in the first place. And what did it matter if she was? She'd pretty much tricked him into marrying her. Maybe she would go after Bernard. Would serve him right.

But if she *was* with Bernard, she was on her way to Montana.

"The sheriff ask you any questions about Jasmine's disappearance?" Bernard asked.

"No. Why would he with her being alive?"

"Because this isn't over. Maybe Jasmine is alive. Maybe she's faking amnesia. Or maybe not. Either way, you think the sheriff is going to stop looking for the person who hid her car in that barn? And now you've got some bartender after you?"

"Not just me. The bartender remembered you, too."

"We'll talk when I get there. The sheriff said the state investigators were still searching the farm."

"They are. I saw lights out there as I was driving here, to the bar. They don't know that Jasmine is alive yet."

"Go back to the motel and stay there. You've done enough damage for one night." Bernard hung up.

Kerrington thought he couldn't feel any worse. He wished he hadn't called Bernard, hadn't told him a damned thing. He wished he had a drink. He wished he'd worn a coat. He was cold. And depressed as hell. He rolled up the window. It was colder here than in Georgia.

He tried his home number, left a message for Sandra to call him on his cell and hung up, wondering if she was on the plane with Bernard. Or if she was sitting in the living room refusing to pick up the phone.

He had no choice. He'd have to go back to the motel. Idly he wondered what time T.C. got off work and what would happen if he was waiting for her in the parking lot.

Somewhere over the Midwest

"WHAT'S GOING ON?" Sandra said, putting down the magazine she'd been reading as Bernard came back into the airplane cabin.

She was sitting in one of the comfortable chairs, her long legs crossed, that same rabid-dog look on her face that she'd had when he'd boarded his company jet and found her waiting for him.

"I'm going with you," she'd said.

"What are you going to tell Kerrington?"

"I don't give a damn *what* you tell him. I'm hitching a ride. Plain and simple."

Nothing was ever plain and simple when it came to Sandra. He'd wanted to argue, list all the reasons this was a really bad idea. But he'd seen by her expression that she was going. He could have had her thrown off, but he wasn't stupid enough to think that wouldn't have massive repercussions.

"That was Kerrington who called you, wasn't it?" she said eyeing him. "Why else would you leave the room?"

Business. A woman. Any number of reasons. But he wasn't up to arguing with her.

"Good news," he said sarcastically. "Kerrington says he just saw Jasmine." He knew the effect that would have on her. He took a sick pleasure in it when Sandra turned the color of skim milk.

"What?"

"He says she's alive."

"How is that possible?" Sandra asked, her voice a hoarse whisper.

Bernard shook his head and considered telling her the rest. But bringing up a bartender from a place where Kerrington met Jasmine in secret didn't seem the wise thing to do. Not if Bernard wanted any peace and quiet on this trip.

Sandra already looked stunned from the other news. He decided to leave well enough alone.

But as he sat back down, he gritted his teeth just thinking about Kerrington. The damned fool had done more stupid things in his life than anyone Bernard had ever known, starting with marrying Sandra.

Now he had a bartender who could place him with Jasmine on the day she disappeared. A bartender who had also seen Bernard that day.

Antelope Flats, Montana

CASH WANTED HER to see Jasmine's car?

Molly swallowed, trying to think of a good reason it would be a bad idea. Wasn't it bad enough to steal the woman's identity—even temporarily and for a good cause? Molly was pretty sure that Jasmine had died in that car. Talk about bad karma.

"Is there some reason you wouldn't want to see the car?" Cash asked.

Molly nodded and put down her fork, her appetite suddenly gone. "I'm afraid."

"Of remembering?"

"Just the thought of seeing the car terrifies me," she said truthfully. "But if you feel it's necessary…"

He shook his head. "It can wait. Maybe we'll go out to the ranch early tomorrow. Do you know how to ride a horse?"

Had Jasmine? She hesitated. "I love horses and have ridden some." At once she saw his surprise. Wrong answer?

"You didn't ride seven years ago. In fact, you said you didn't like horses," he said, studying her.

She raised a brow. "More proof I'm not Jasmine. Or maybe I changed my mind."

"Maybe. But it's good that you ride. We have several gentle mares and we wouldn't go far. From horseback is the best way to see the ranch."

"I'm looking forward to it," she said truthfully.

From what she had gathered, the Sundown Ranch was a good ways outside of town. Which meant there was little chance of running into anyone she was supposed to have known.

He smiled. "Good. Let's just have a nice day tomorrow and not worry about anything. How does that sound?"

"Heavenly. Thank you." She wondered why he'd let her off the hook so easily. It didn't matter. She felt as if she'd been given time off, but maybe that's exactly what Cash *wanted* her to think.

She'd felt him studying her during the meal and several times caught him frowning. Tomorrow could be a trap. She'd be a fool to let down her guard. And then there was his mother.

Still, she thought even Shelby McCall was a better bet than Jasmine's brother Bernard. She hoped to put off that encounter as long as possible.

"Did you have enough to eat?"

She nodded and groaned. "Are you kidding? It was the best meal I've ever had."

He laughed, not realizing she really meant it as he shoved back his chair and began clearing the dishes.

She stood as well and took her plate over to the sink. "Dinner was amazing. Thank you again."

He didn't look at her as he began to rinse the dishes

and put them in the dishwasher. The old-fashioned kitchen felt cozy and warm, rich with the wonderful smells of dinner. She noticed that he'd made some improvements in here, unlike the rest of the downstairs.

Her gaze lit on his face and she experienced a jolt. Was that a guilty conscience she'd felt? Whatever it was, it made her uncomfortable. She dropped her gaze.

He put soap in the dishwasher and started it. "I could make us some coffee…."

"Not for me, thanks."

"Don't you drink coffee?" he asked.

Immediately she saw that this was a test. Jasmine must have loved coffee.

Well, too bad. She hated coffee and she wasn't drinking it. "I don't like the taste."

"Jasmine didn't like coffee either," he said, surprising her. "At least not unless it was a latte or something that hid the actual taste of the coffee."

Molly said nothing, feeling as if she'd just dodged a bullet.

"I didn't ask you if you'd like dessert. I have some fudge brownies—"

"Please. Don't tempt me." She grinned, licked her lips just thinking about brownies and realized he was staring at her mouth and frowning. "So was it love at first sight?" she asked quickly, wondering if there was something about her mouth that was giving her away.

"What?" He jerked his gaze up to her eyes.

"You and Jasmine, was it love at first sight?"

"Something like that," he said. His gaze settled over her, making her feel too warm. "You must be tired."

She nodded. "It's been quite the day."

"Why don't we talk tomorrow on the way out to the ranch?" he said. "It's been quite the day for me as well."

"I'm sorry I have so many questions."

He shook his head. "It's understandable. I can't imagine what it must be like for you, not knowing who you are."

She nodded, feeling more like a fake than ever. "You're right, I *am* tired."

"I put some towels out in the bathroom," he said.

Suddenly the option of sinking into that claw-foot tub up to her neck in bubbles was all she could think about. "Thank you. For everything." She met his pale blue eyes. They reminded her of bright sunny mornings, clear blue skies and the short periods she'd felt happy in her life.

"My pleasure. Please let me know if you need anything." He seemed to hesitate. "Good night...Molly. I can't tell you how glad I am that you saw that photograph in the paper and came here."

She smiled, wondering if he would feel that way when the fingerprint results came back. "Good night."

But as she started to turn away, she saw him move toward her. Her body anticipated his touch, warming, skin instantly hypersensitive, pulse pounding, a breath catching in her throat.

His fingers brushed her arm, turning her back to face him. He looked into her eyes and she felt something inside her melt as if touched to a flame.

She'd promised herself she wouldn't let him kiss her. A lover's kiss would give her away faster than fingerprint results from the FBI.

But she couldn't move, couldn't breathe, couldn't bear the thought that he might change his mind.

He cupped her cheek with one hand, his eyes never leaving hers as he drew her closer. His other arm slipped around her, pulling her to him.

She looked into all that blue, lost in the wonderful feel of being sheltered in his arms. She could feel the thump of his heart beneath the soft fabric of his uniform shirt as he drew her closer.

He leaned toward her. She should have drawn back. She should have stopped him.

His mouth dropped to hers. There was nothing tentative about his kiss. It was a lover's kiss, full of pleasure and passion, desire and heat. Her lips parted, opening to him, her body alive with sensation.

It felt so right being in his arms that she forgot who she was. Forgot her promise not to let this happen. Forgot that he thought he was holding Jasmine, the woman he'd loved, not her. Not Molly Kilpatrick.

She pulled back. She was starting to believe her own lies, starting to care for a man who was in love with a ghost. "I…I'm not Jasmine." Her voice broke and she felt hot tears. What was wrong with her?

"No," he said, his voice rough with emotion as he let go of her and stepped back. "You're Molly. Molly Kilpatrick."

She stared at him, her eyes burning with tears. At that moment she would have given anything to be Jasmine. She swallowed, realizing the horrible mistake she'd made. He had to have known that she wasn't the woman she was pretending to be. The kiss had given her away.

"I'm sorry," he said.

No sorrier than her. She waited for him to call her on her lie. He knew now that she wasn't Jasmine, didn't he?

"I promised myself I wouldn't do that," he said.

She nodded slowly, unable to speak.

"Please say you'll still go with me out to the ranch tomorrow. I won't kiss you again."

He still wanted to take her to his family ranch?

"I wanted you to kiss me," she said.

He raised a brow.

"I had hoped it might trigger a memory," she said quickly. She was tired. And foolish. And she couldn't remember the last time a man had kissed her like that.

"But the kiss didn't trigger anything?"

She shook her head, waiting for him to say something about the kiss. He didn't.

"Good night again," he said instead. "Let me know if you need anything. I'm just right down the hall."

"Good night." She hurried to her room before he could see how shaken she was.

The kiss had stirred surprising emotions in her. She didn't want to feel anything for Cash McCall. It was bad enough what she was doing to him by pretending to be Jasmine. She didn't want to start liking the man. Or worse.

Too late for that. Who wouldn't have liked him? He was a nice guy.

All the more reason not to get any more involved than necessary.

She'd known it wouldn't be easy, pulling this off. But she hadn't expected Cash McCall. Not this gentle, loving cowboy who'd waited seven years for the woman he loved.

She could just hear her father saying that Cash was nothing but a small-town sheriff. How wrong her father would be. There was more to Cash McCall than any man she'd ever met. And he was in love with the woman she was pretending to be. Just her luck.

And as luck would have it, he was also the kind of man who wouldn't take being duped lying down.

CASH WASN'T SURE what had awakened him at first. He'd had a terrible time getting to sleep, unable to forget the kiss and the emotions it had evoked.

He'd thought once he kissed her, he would know for certain whether or not she was Jasmine. Instead, the kiss had only further confused him. He hadn't expected to *feel* anything. Not after seven years. Not after everything that had happened.

But he'd *felt* more than just something. The kiss had knocked him off his feet. He had never felt anything like it. Certainly not with Jasmine.

But if this woman *was* Jasmine, what kind of sense did that make? Even more to the point, what if she was a complete stranger who evoked this kind of passion with her kisses like no woman he'd ever known?

He heard a floorboard creak outside his door. Old houses settled constantly. He'd come to know the house's unique sounds. This wasn't one of them.

He quit trying to identify the woman he'd kissed and slipped on his jeans. Whomever she was, she was up, walking around his house.

This woman had…passion. He realized that was the word that best described her. She not only had passion, she also stirred it in him. That made her very dangerous, he realized.

Another floorboard creaked. She was headed down the hallway. He stood perfectly still, listening as the footsteps retreated down the hall toward the stairs.

He waited until he heard the third stair from the top groan, then moved quietly to the door. Carefully, he opened it and looked out just in time to catch a glimpse of her blond head in the moonlight from the window over the stairs.

Maybe she was going downstairs to get a drink of water. Or find those brownies he'd told her about earlier.

Or maybe she was looking for something.

He sneaked down the hall in the dark, trying to avoid the spots on the floor that creaked.

A lower step creaked under her weight. He slowed at the top of the stairs and waited for her to finish her descent. From where he stood out of the light, he could see her dark shadow creeping down the remaining steps as if trying hard to be quiet.

He waited to see which way she went next, hoping she would head for the kitchen and the brownies.

Instead she moved down the hall to his den.

He frowned. Maybe she was sleepwalking and didn't know where she was going.

Right.

She opened the den door and quickly stepped inside. He descended the stairs, stepping over the creaky ones. A thin gold line of light shone under the den door by the time he reached it.

He didn't think sleepwalkers turned on lights or

closed doors or made phone calls. He could hear her dialing the phone. She either didn't have a cell phone or it didn't work in Antelope Flats.

He listened but heard only the click of the phone as she hung up.

The light went out under the door. He hurried back down the hall to duck into the dark living room, flattening himself against the wall where he had a view of part of the hallway, the opening to the dark kitchen and the stairs.

She stopped at the entrance to the kitchen as if undecided about something. He heard her say, "No," firmly, then start up the stairs.

He held his breath, afraid she would turn and see him, knowing he would have no explanation for sneaking around in his own house. Her call could have been innocent. Uh-huh.

She didn't get far up the stairs when she stopped, sighed, looked down at her feet and shook her head, then turned and came back down the steps. She disappeared into the dark kitchen.

The light came on. He heard her opening and closing cabinet doors, obviously trying to be quiet. She was looking for the brownies.

He smiled in spite of his concern about the phone call. He heard her find the brownies and the silverware. He heard her open the fridge, pour a glass of milk, close the carton and pull out a chair at the kitchen table.

He peeked around the corner. She was sitting at the kitchen table, her back to him. He eased his way out of his hiding place and crept up the stairs, the sight of her branded into his memory.

Molly sitting cross-legged on the chair in her baby-doll pajamas, her blond hair still wet from her bath, her feet bare, her toes painted with pale pink polish, her legs tanned and long. Nothing about her reminded him of Jasmine just then. And he was surprised that it didn't upset him.

The cop in him reminded that she'd just sneaked down to make a phone call in the middle of the night. His smile faded. The woman had a secret. Probably more than one.

He hurried to his room. A few minutes later, he heard her return to hers. He could assume she was in for the night. He picked up the extension in his bedroom and hit Redial.

A long-distance number came up on the caller ID screen. He waited as the number rang.

"You've reached the answering machine of Lanny Giliano. Can't come to the phone right now. Leave a message. I'll get back to you."

He hung up and checked the area code. Las Vegas, Nevada. That's where she'd said she'd been most recently.

And apparently she'd called a man there. Of course there would be a man in her life, he thought ruefully. Especially if she was Jasmine.

Chapter Ten

Friday
Antelope Flats, Montana

Molly woke to the smell of fresh-perked coffee and cinnamon rolls and the sound of a soft tap on her door after the best night of sleep she'd ever had.

It helped that she hadn't had to get up early to evacuate the room so she wasn't caught by some energetic hotel maid. The brownie and glass of milk she'd eaten in the middle of the night hadn't hurt either.

But her call to Lanny had produced no news. Had the police found him? Was it possible he was still alive?

She'd climbed into the bed last night, the sheets smelling of sunshine, after soaking in the claw-foot tub and had dropped right off. Her last thought before she'd fallen asleep was Cash, followed quickly by the admonition, *Don't get used to this.*

Then she'd woken in the middle of the night thinking about Lanny. Needing to know what was happening. Last night though, she'd just hung up, afraid she'd made a mistake calling Lanny's again.

She sat up now, pulling the covers to her chin. "Come in," she called. Her heart took off at the memory of their kiss, but she rounded it back up. *Remember, he thinks you're Jasmine.*

The door opened and he came in with a tray. A cup of coffee for himself, a large glass of milk for her and two huge warm cinnamon rolls cut in slices and buttered. There was also a small bouquet of flowers.

She couldn't help the smile that burst out at the sight of him—and the tray of food and flowers. No one had ever brought her breakfast in bed. Certainly no one who ever looked like Cash McCall. This was like a dream she never wanted to wake up from.

He dragged up a chair. "Sleep well?"

She nodded eagerly, feeling only a little guilty about her middle-of-the-night phone call. She wanted to tell him the truth, hated that she was deceiving him. But she couldn't chance that Vince and Angel were still on the loose and looking for her. And she didn't want to leave here. Not yet.

He handed her the glass of milk and she helped herself to one of the slices of cinnamon rolls. She groaned, closing her eyes and licking her lips. She heard his soft laugh and opened her eyes again.

"My sister-in-law Cassidy made those," he said of the cinnamon rolls. "She owns the Longhorn Café. Best cook around."

She heard the admiration in his voice. "She's married to your brother…."

"Rourke. They just got back from their honeymoon." He looked down into his coffee cup as if uncomfortable. If Jasmine hadn't disappeared he would have been married now too.

They ate in a companionable silence. It felt odd having a man in her bedroom. Probably because it had been so long since she'd even had a date. And then there was that kiss they'd shared last night. She'd sworn she'd seen fireworks.

She studied him from under her lashes, worried that after the kiss last night he knew she wasn't Jasmine.

But as they finished the rolls and he drained his coffee cup, he rose and said, "I thought we'd head out to the ranch this morning as soon as you're ready." He seemed shy, hesitant.

She flashed him a smile. "Thank you for breakfast. It was wonderful. I've never had breakfast in bed before." She caught herself. "At least not that I can remember."

He smiled. "I'll see you downstairs. Wear something comfortable."

When she was dressed in jeans, a shirt and tennis shoes, she went down. "Cash?" No answer. "Cash?"

As she passed the closed den door, she heard him in there on the phone. She wanted to get a hat she'd left in her car. The garage was separate from the house, so she opened the front door and stepped out.

The day was beautiful, the sky crystalline blue, the mountains in the distance snowcapped. Closer, a breeze stirred the boughs of the pines around the house. From here, she couldn't even see another house, and only the glimpses of other buildings toward town through more trees.

She walked out to the garage and had just started to open the door when she heard someone behind her.

Turning, she came face-to-face with Kerrington. She hadn't seen his car. But she should have smelled his cologne. It was a nauseating scent that had mixed with his sweat. He looked as if he had either slept in his clothes or hadn't been to bed at all.

"We need to talk," he said gruffly. "The sheriff isn't here, so you can drop the act." He glanced toward the house, then grabbed her arm and pulled her to the side of the garage, away from the house under a large old pine.

Beyond the trees there was nothing on this side of the house but open land to the west, red sandy bluffs, sagebrush and a few dark pines against the horizon. A thought sped by: could Cash hear her in the house if she screamed?

"What did you tell him?" Kerrington demanded, her unease growing at the agitated look in his eyes.

"What?" Cash would have no idea where she'd gone. And Kerrington was scaring her.

"I didn't sleep at all last night," he said as if it were her fault.

She'd slept like a baby, once she'd put the kiss out of her mind. And once she'd had that brownie and milk. "What is it you want?"

"When are you going to tell him?"

"I don't know what you're talking about."

"About us," he snapped.

Us? "I told you. I'm not Jasmine and I don't know what you're talking about." He was obviously angry and she didn't like being alone with him. She started to step past him but he grabbed her arm and jerked her to him. She slammed into his chest, his grip on her arm tightening.

"You and I both know your…engagement to Cash McCall was a sham and not the romantic love story that's been in all the papers," Kerrington said with a sneer. "You were seeing me behind the sheriff's back. You love *me*."

Jasmine had been having an affair with Kerrington while engaged to Cash? "I don't believe you," she snapped, jerking her arm free and stepping back from him.

"There is no one here but the two of us," he said, almost pleading now. "What's going on. Please, Jasmine." His gaze met hers and Molly saw pain there. He really had loved Jasmine. Was it possible Jasmine had felt the same way about him? "You can't have forgotten what we had together."

An affair. Behind Cash's back. That part she saw wasn't a lie. She felt sick with the knowledge. "I'm not Jasmine. Now, let me pass."

"You're making a big mistake," he said through gritted teeth as he stepped closer.

"You're the one making the mistake," said a rough-edged male voice behind Kerrington.

Kerrington whirled around, his face blanching at the sight of Sheriff Cash McCall behind him. He stepped back, obviously seeing the fierceness in Cash's eyes, the set of his jaw, the clenched fist.

"Jasmine and I were just…talking," Kerrington said.

"Really? It almost sounded as if you were threatening her," Cash said. A muscle jumped in his jaw and Molly could see that it was taking every ounce of restraint in him not to attack Kerrington physically.

He shot her a glance. "Are you all right?"

She nodded, but he would have been a fool not to see

that she was shaken. And Cash McCall, she was learning, was no fool. She wondered how much of the conversation he'd overheard. And hated the thought that he might have heard about the affair.

Cash turned to Kerrington again. "I think you'd better leave."

Kerrington nodded in agreement and shot her a look she couldn't read. She just knew she didn't want to meet him in a dark alley. He turned and walked down the street toward Main Street without looking back.

A silence fell between her and Cash. She didn't know what to say. But she could see that he was still angry. She prayed he hadn't overheard all of their conversation. He'd loved Jasmine. Hadn't been able to move on with his life even after all this time. She couldn't bear the thought of him being hurt. Especially by Kerrington.

She couldn't help but think about what Cash had said about Jasmine leaving the gas station with someone she knew. Kerrington? Had he gotten away with murder?

If that was the case, no wonder he was so upset at seeing a woman he thought was Jasmine.

Molly was beginning to realize the danger she'd put herself in. Kerrington believed she was Jasmine. Was it possible that if he'd thought he'd killed Jasmine, that he might do just as Cash has feared and try to finish the job before she remembered?

She shivered, remembering the look in Kerrington's eyes.

"Are you ready?" Cash asked, none of the usual warmth or concern in his voice.

With a shock, she realized he was angry with her. He thought she was Jasmine. How much had he heard? She wanted to deny everything, deny she was Jasmine, but she realized right then he wouldn't have believed her even if she had confessed everything.

"I just need to get my hat out of my car," she said, feeling sick with shame for an affair she'd never had, for hurting a man she found herself caring about more and more all the time.

"I'll get it for you," he said and disappeared into the garage.

She leaned against the garage wall, miserable with what she'd learned. Cash had definitely fallen in love with the wrong woman. Is that why his mother had reacted to her the way she had? Did she know about Jasmine's affair with Kerrington?

And now they were headed out to the ranch. Molly groaned inwardly. She'd put herself in danger on all fronts. What did she expect pretending to be another woman? This had turned out to be even more reckless than she'd first thought. And heartbreaking as well, she thought as Cash came out with her hat.

CASH WAS STILL SHAKING with anger as he loaded a small picnic basket into his newer model red pickup. He tried not to think about Kerrington or the phone call he'd had just moments before that.

He'd wanted to hit Kerrington. But it wasn't the first time and he doubted it would be the last.

He hadn't heard Jasmine leave the house. He'd been on the phone with State Investigator John Mathews. Mathews had called to tell him that he was being relieved as sheriff pending the conclusion of the investigation.

"You're taking this better than I expected," Mathews had said.

Cash had wanted to tell him that Jasmine might be alive. But he heard himself say, "Not much I can do about it. With luck, the case will be solved soon."

Mathews had cleared his throat and Cash had known there was more coming. He had held his breath, afraid Mathews would tell him that they'd found Jasmine's body.

"There was a murder. Coroner puts it at about 4:00 a.m. The bartender out at the Mello Dee."

With a shock, Cash had realized he hadn't been called. So he'd been relieved of his duties yesterday and Mathews just hadn't told him.

"Name was Teresa Clark. You know her?" Mathews had asked.

For a moment, Cash had wondered if he was a suspect in her murder, too. Then he'd realized that the question was a normal one given that he was from here and Mathews was out of Billings, hours away.

"No, but I heard the Mello Dee had sold and was under new management," he'd said.

"We'll be investigating the murder, along with still searching the farm for…remains." Remains.

Cash had said nothing, waiting for what had to be coming next.

"That blue paint chip you took from Jasmine Wolfe's car," Mathews had said. "The lab says it's from a Ford pickup. I believe you drove a blue Ford pickup seven years ago."

Cash had closed his eyes. "A lot of people drove blue Ford pickups seven years ago. It must have been their most popular color."

Mathews had said nothing. "Where can I reach you if I need to talk to you?"

"Just give me a call on my cell phone. I'm not going anywhere."

Mathews had sounded relieved to hear that.

As Cash had hung up, he'd caught a glimpse of Kerrington through the window. By the time he reached the front door, Kerrington was dragging Jasmine around the side of the garage.

Cash raked a hand through his hair now and swore, remembering what he'd overhead.

Molly came up behind him. He didn't turn. Didn't want to face her right now. What he'd heard between her and Kerrington had him too upset and he didn't want her to see that. Didn't want her to know what he was feeling right now.

"Cash?"

He felt her hand on his back, the heat coursing through him to his core. He took a breath and let it out slowly before he finally turned and forced himself to smile. "We couldn't have picked a more beautiful day for a horseback ride around the ranch."

MOLLY TRIED TO RELAX as she climbed into the front seat of Cash's pickup. They wouldn't be taking the patrol car.

She was thankful for that, thinking this way they would attract less attention.

Cash was still upset. He was trying to hide it, but she'd been reading people for too much of her life not to see it. She was torn with a need to warn Cash that she believed Kerrington might have killed Jasmine —and yet not give herself away.

"I was thinking about what you said yesterday about Jasmine not getting into a car except with someone she knew," Molly said carefully.

He shot her a look. "You think she got into the car with Kerrington."

"He is so angry."

Cash didn't drive downtown, but seemed to wander the gravel backstreets, coming out on the edge of town on Main Street, as if he didn't want to be seen. Didn't want her to be seen.

Molly slumped down a little in the seat, not wanting another confrontation this morning. If they could just get out of town—

"He does seem awfully angry with Jasmine," Cash said without looking at her. "Any idea what that is about?"

Not a clue since she wasn't Jasmine.

"I just thought I should warn you," she said.

He looked over at her and smiled. "Thanks for your concern."

She couldn't tell if he was being sincere or not. She shut up and looked out the window, worried what Kerrington would do next.

As Cash turned onto the main highway, Molly looked up and saw a car driving slowly into town. She spotted the Nevada license plates first. Her gaze flew to the two men behind the windshield. Vince and Angel.

Her heart dropped. They'd found her? She flung herself forward, pretending she'd dropped something, as the car slowly passed them. Had they seen her?

"Are you all right?" Cash asked.

"Fine. I just dropped my…lipstick on the floor." Vince and Angel were in town. It was impossible. Even if they'd followed her…. Not that it mattered. All that mattered was that they'd found her—and she had to disappear and quickly.

She had a tube of lip gloss in her purse. Bent over, she did a sleight of hand, and straightened, the gloss in her fingers. She held it up, smiled foolishly. "Got it."

As she leaned back, she checked the side mirror. The car had turned in to the Longhorn Café.

"Darn," Cash said. "I forgot. I need to run one quick errand before we go out to the ranch. You don't mind do you?"

SHE DID MIND. Cash could see fear in her expression, the same fear he'd seen when she'd spotted the car. Her skin had blanched white under her tan. She looked as if she'd seen a ghost or worse. Nor had he been fooled by why she'd ducked down as the two men had driven by. Nevada plates. Didn't she say she'd been in Las Vegas?

He'd quickly glanced in his side mirror and memorized the license plate number as she'd bent to retrieve her lipstick. He hadn't seen where she'd pulled it from, but he was positive she hadn't dropped it.

"I just need to talk to my sister-in-law for minute,"

he said, swinging the pickup around. The two men had gotten out of the car with the Nevada plates and were headed into the Longhorn Café. One was big, the other short and wiry-looking. "I told you she owns the only café in town."

He thought Jasmine might have a heart attack.

"The café?" she said a little breathlessly, looking down the street as the two men disappeared inside the café. That was definitely fear in her expression. No mistaking it. Who were the men? And why was she was so frightened of them?

"Why don't I drop you by the house," he said. "I'm not sure how long this will take. I'm sorry."

She was so relieved, he almost felt guilty for letting her think he was taking her to the café where the two men had gone. Almost. What was she hiding from him? Something to do with the men. Well, he would find out soon enough.

He stopped in front of the house. "The door's open. I won't be long. I promise."

She smiled and got out. "Don't hurry on my account."

Would she try to take off while he was gone?

"Oh, shoot, I need to get something from the garage first." He got out. "Make yourself at home." He waited. She stood for a moment on the sidewalk then headed for the house. He waited until she was inside before he stepped into the garage to make sure her car wasn't going anywhere.

MOLLY COULDN'T QUIT SHAKING. Vince and Angel were in town. How could they have found her? Not that it mattered. She had to get away. *Now.*

She hurried upstairs, threw her few belongings into her suitcase and carried it downstairs. Peering out the front window, she saw with a sigh of relief that Cash hadn't returned. She felt awful running out on him like this. She would call him when she was far enough away he couldn't find her. Not that he'd come looking for her—once she told him the truth.

Opening the door, she stepped out with her suitcase and turned to close the door behind her.

"Going somewhere?" asked a voice behind her.

CASH PARKED HIS PICKUP behind the Longhorn Café and hurried in through the back door. His sister-in-law's office was just inside. He stepped into it and waited to catch her attention, motioning her to join him.

"Two men just came into the café. I need their prints," he said without preamble. He'd known Cassidy his whole life. He'd always thought of her as a sister, which was fortunate since she'd been in love with his brother Rourke since the two were kids.

Cassidy smiled and lifted a brow. "Okay. Nice to see you too, Cash. The honeymoon? Oh, it was wonderful. Your brother Rourke? He's fine."

"Sorry. I don't have much time."

"It's okay." Her smile faded. "I heard the news about Jasmine's car being found. I'm sorry."

He nodded.

"So let me guess which two men you want prints on," she said. She described the two who'd just come in. "Both look like they've had some time to lift weights not to mention the prison tattoos."

Cash wasn't surprised. "Get me their prints if you can on anything they touch. I'll stop by later. Thanks. I really appreciate this. I wouldn't ask but—"

"No need to explain. We're family," she said. "Any time you need *anything...*"

He smiled. "Thanks." He couldn't wait to get back to Jasmine but he had to make one more stop. His office. There was a chance Frank might have faxed him the fingerprint results.

He rolled down his window, needing the fresh air to collect his thoughts as he drove the few blocks to his office. He wanted to rush back to the house and make her tell him about the men at the café. And the phone call she'd made last night. He wanted to demand answers. But part of him was afraid she would tell him that she wasn't Jasmine, and that was something he didn't want to hear. Not yet.

One thing was clear. Whomever this woman was, she was in some kind of trouble. But was she in trouble because she was Jasmine? Or because she wasn't?

MOLLY SPUN AROUND TO SEE a tall, slim woman with long dark hair pulled back from a pale, narrow face. Beside her was a smaller woman with mousy-brown hair done in a style much too old for her. She seemed to be standing back as if almost afraid.

"Well," the taller of the two said on a hasty breath. "You really *are* alive."

Molly couldn't miss the knife edge to her voice. "I'm sorry, do I know you?"

The woman laughed. "I heard you were having trouble remembering. I'm Sandra. Your best friend."

The way Sandra said it, Molly assumed Sandra and Jasmine had been anything *but* best friends.

"And this is Patty Franklin," she said dismissively. "We were your roommates."

Molly looked at Patty, then Sandra. "I'm afraid you've gotten the wrong impression…."

"Cut the crap and invite us in," Sandra said and looked toward the door to the house. "You're not going anywhere."

Molly looked into Sandra's face and saw that she would do whatever it took to keep her from leaving. Picking up her suitcase from where she'd set it on the porch, Molly pushed open the door, seeing no way to avoid this. Telling the women she wasn't Jasmine wouldn't do the trick. No one believed her. Molly had done too good of a job becoming Jasmine.

Once in the living room, Molly motioned to the bar and Sandra poured herself a drink, then lit a cigarette. Patty stood, looking nervous and unsure. Molly hurried to find something Sandra could use as an ashtray. If she could get rid of the women before Cash returned—

"Okay, let's have it," Sandra snapped, then took a drag on her cigarette, glaring at her through the smoke as she exhaled.

"I beg your pardon?" Molly said.

"What is it you want? Kerrington? He's yours. Half Bernard's money? Get a good lawyer, but I'm sure you can have that, too. What else can we give you?" Sandra sounded close to tears, which surprised Molly.

"I don't want anything."

Sandra laughed again, a sharp painful sound. "Oh,

you *always* want something. Usually something someone else has."

Molly looked over at Patty. "Did you all hate Jasmine that much?" She couldn't hide her surprise or horror.

Sandra narrowed her gaze again. "Are we back to you pretending you're not Jasmine again?"

"I know I look like Jasmine but my name is Molly. Molly Kilpatrick."

Sandra sneered at her. "Can we just be honest with each other for a minute? It's just us girls."

"Okay," Molly said. "Why don't you start with telling me why someone would want me dead?"

Sandra laughed. "You don't know? You play with people's lives for your own amusement."

"Kerrington," Molly guessed.

Sandra stiffened. "You don't love him. You never did. You just didn't want me to have him."

"I'm sorry."

Sandra's eyes were bright and hard with tears. She shook her head as if she didn't believe her.

"Look, the sheriff sent off my fingerprints so they can be compared with Jasmine's," Molly said. "We'll know in a week or so if I'm Jasmine. But I can tell you right now, I'm not. I don't expect you to believe me," she continued before Sandra could argue the point. "But you have nothing to fear from me. I don't want Kerrington or Bernard's money or…" She looked at Patty, having almost forgotten about her. The woman looked scared and Molly wondered what she feared Jasmine might want from her. "Or to hurt any of you."

"If what you say is true, and these fingerprint results

will be back in a week and prove you aren't Jasmine," Sandra said, "then where are you taking off to in such a hurry?"

"I have some personal business I need to take care of, which has to do with me being Molly Kilpatrick—not Jasmine Wolfe," she said honestly.

"Right. Whatever you're up to, Jazz, we aren't going to let you destroy our lives," Sandra said. "Not anymore. Don't try to leave town. We're going to finish this before any of us leave, understand?"

Sandra's threat might have scared her if Molly didn't have two felons after her—one who loved to cut up people.

"Let's go, Patty," Sandra said. Patty hadn't uttered a word the entire time.

As the women left, Molly heard Cash's pickup pull up out front. She groaned and hurriedly stashed her suitcase behind the couch.

As Sandra and Patty left, Molly saw them pass Cash on the walk. He turned to watch them get into a silver rental sedan and drive away, then turned to see her standing on the porch.

"I guess the word is out," he said. "You all right?"

She nodded. What did it matter if everyone found out about her now? Vince and Angel had already found her. "Sandra and Patty, roommates of Jasmine's, just wanted to stop by for a talk."

"And?" He looked worried.

"They think I want something from them. They just don't know what yet."

His look said he thought the same thing. "Ready to

go? It's about ten miles out to the ranch," he said, as if he suspected there was nothing she wanted more than to distance herself from here right now.

"Great," she said. "I'm ready." This wasn't what she'd planned when she'd packed her suitcase, but at least she would get out of town for a day. Then tonight, when Cash was asleep, she would retrieve her suitcase from behind the couch and leave.

Chapter Eleven

Molly rolled down her window as Cash had done, letting the wind whip at her short hair. She closed her eyes and tried to breathe. The late morning air chilled her. She tried to calm down, to think.

Vince and Angel were in town. They'd found her. Or at least found out what town she was in—and given the size of Antelope Flats, it wouldn't be long before they knew where she was hiding.

She couldn't believe what a mess she'd made of things. Antelope Flats was the one place she'd never expected to be found. Nor that she was jeopardizing Cash's life just by being with him. She had to leave as soon as possible.

She thought about telling him the truth. But why would he believe her? He was convinced she was Jasmine. As sheriff, he could keep her from leaving, thinking he could protect her. She wouldn't endanger his life. Even Cash McCall was no match for Vince and Angel.

"That's the Tongue River Reservoir," Cash said as the pickup climbed a long hill.

She looked in the direction he'd pointed and saw the pool of blue against the red rock bluffs. "It's beautiful."

"The legend is Native Americans named the river the Tongue because of the way it winds."

Like a forked tongue, she thought, as the rolling countryside blurred past. The air smelled of summer and water, sage and pine. Wild grasses ran bright green to silver sage. On the rocky bluffs, dark green pine trees stood against the clear blue of the summer sky.

She tried to relax. They would be safe at the ranch, then tonight as soon as Cash was asleep —

"Those are the Bighorn Mountains," Cash said, pointing in the other direction.

The mountains were the same snowcapped ones she'd seen from his house this morning. They stretched across the horizon, deep purple except for the snow-covered tips.

"We run our cattle on summer range up there," he said as he turned onto a dirt road.

"How many cows do you have?"

"That's something you never ask a rancher."

"I'm sorry," she said quickly and he laughed.

"It's all right. I don't mind. We run about a thousand head and still keep longhorns mostly just for tradition since they were what the ranch was started with. Our main herd is Herefords."

She heard the pride in his voice. "I'm surprised you became a sheriff instead of staying on the ranch."

"Oh, I still help ranch. It's in my blood," he said. "But I needed to do my own thing." He was silent after that.

She stared out at the land. What could keep a person

here where there was little more than rocks and trees? Just inertia. That's what Max had always said kept most men in one place. Laziness or inertia. "They just don't know or want any better."

Not that moving around had seemed to make her life better or her father's. But it did fight boredom. She feared she would grow stagnant if she stayed too long in one place. But then she didn't seem to belong anywhere.

Dust boiled up behind them as the road trailed alongside a sparkling creek. The water rushed in a tumble of white spray through large boulders, pooling dark in eddies, hedged in by bright red bushes.

"That's Rosebud Creek," Cash said. "Those are wild rosebushes growing along the edge. The taller trees are cottonwoods and willows."

"What are those?" she asked.

"The red? Dogwood. The other bushes are chokecherry trees. By the end of August the branches will be heavy with fruit."

She looked over at him, hearing a kind of reverence in his voice. "How long have you lived here?"

He laughed. "I was born here. So was my father. As I mentioned last night, my grandfather brought one of the first herds of longhorn cattle to Montana from Texas. The minute he saw this land, he knew he'd found his home."

What was it like to have roots that ran that deep? As she looked out at the countryside, she tried to imagine being one of the first white men to see this. The landscape looked inhospitable to her. She couldn't imagine fighting to tame even a small part of it for a home.

"Was your grandfather married?" she asked, unable

to see a woman wanting to live this far away from civilization even now let alone a hundred years ago.

Cash laughed at her question. "Not at the time." He was smiling at her.

"What?"

"You're trying to imagine why anyone would live out here."

She started to deny it, then laughed. "Sorry. I've always lived in cities."

"At least the part of your life you remember," he said.

She realized her mistake. "Yes."

As they came over a rise, he said, "There's the ranch." He drove under a huge log entry that read: Sundown Ranch.

She remembered the old cabin she'd seen in the photograph last night in the hallway at his house. But what she saw instead made her catch her breath. A cluster of buildings, the barns red-roofed, the house at the center rambling and huge, scattered across a grass carpet.

The ranch house was built of logs, just like the first homestead, but these logs were massive and golden in the sun. There was a tan rock chimney that towered up one side and a porch that ran across the entire front of the house.

She remembered the photograph she'd seen on Cash's desk, the one of his family, and knew it had been shot on that very porch.

The memory, like the ranch house, sparked a yearning she'd never felt before. Not for the ranch or the beautiful home. But for the family. Tears burned her eyes.

She hurriedly wiped at them. "I had no idea it was

so…" She waved a hand through the air, unable to find the right words.

"My father built the house. It's nothing like the places you've lived."

He was right about that—just not in the way he meant, she thought as he pulled into the yard and cut the engine.

She stared at the sprawling two-story, log ranch house with its red tin roof and tried to imagine what it would be like to grow up here, to be raised in a large family like that. It was beyond her imagination.

Through the big window, she could see the wide staircase, almost feel the homey, inviting warmth of the furnishings. She was hit again with that sense of yearning. It felt a lot like the emotion she'd experienced last night when Cash had taken her in his arms and kissed her.

The need to run practically made her throw open her door and take off at a trot. She was just beginning to realize what she'd gotten herself into. Even if Vince and Angel hadn't come to town, she needed to leave. Even if Jasmine's enemies didn't want to kill her again, she needed to distance herself from this place, from these people. She'd thought she would be safe here. She'd been wrong on all counts.

Nothing was safe about getting this close to Cash. Or his family. Her very thoughts weren't safe, let alone the emotions Cash evoked in her. She would leave him a note confessing everything. He wouldn't come after her. She was sure of that. He would be too disgusted.

He had climbed out of the pickup and gone around to open her door for her. She'd been so wrapped up in her thoughts that she'd hardly noticed. But now she felt shy, as if they were on a date, and anxious about meeting his family and seeing his mother again. If she could just get through this day—

"I should warn you," Cash said as he led her up the steps to the porch. "My family can be—" The front door flew open. Molly could hear raised voices as a young woman emerged from the house, slamming the door behind her, then halting in surprise to see them on the porch.

"   a little much," Cash finished. "Dusty?"

The young woman was pretty, dressed in western attire with blond hair pulled back into a ponytail, no makeup, and even paler blue eyes than Cash's.

"Dusty?" he said again.

The young woman's eyes widened at the sight of Jasmine. Obviously Shelby had warned the rest of the family.

"This is Molly," Cash said, as if purposely not calling her Jasmine.

Dusty continued to stare.

Molly could see that Cash's sister was both curious—and protective of her brother.

"But Shelby said—"

Cash made a strangled sound. "She looks like Jasmine but we haven't verified that she is yet. So for simplicity's sake, let's call her Molly."

Molly felt a surge of gratitude toward him. He was trying to protect her. Maybe especially from his mother, and whatever Dusty and Shelby had been just fighting about.

Dusty seemed to make up her own mind. She threw her arms around Molly's neck.

Molly stiffened for a moment in surprise, then raised her arms and embraced the young woman, looking over her shoulder at Cash in surprise.

He groaned again. "Dusty, you're embarrassing her."

Dusty pulled back, her eyes full of tears. "I just know how much my brother loves you, how much he's missed you. Whatever happened in the past, it doesn't matter. The two of you belong together."

Molly felt the full weight of the young woman's words. "Dusty, I might not be Jasmine—"

Dusty smiled and cut her eyes to her brother. "Don't you think Cash would know his own fiancée? The love of his life?"

It would seem so, Cash thought, looking over at Molly. She seemed different today. In fact, when he looked at her, he wondered what had made him so sure she was Jasmine. She was so different from the woman he'd known.

But like Jasmine, this woman had secrets. And that alone almost convinced him she was Jasmine. That and the fact that he needed Jasmine to be alive for strictly selfish reasons.

And by tonight, his friend at the FBI would have called with the fingerprint results.

"What's going on?" he asked Dusty, indicating whatever he and Molly had interrupted.

"*Shelby,*" Dusty said, as if that explained it all.

"I thought the two of you were closer after working on Rourke and Cassidy's wedding," he said.

Dusty rolled her eyes. "Like one wedding is going to change everything?"

He realized it was a subject best dropped as his father appeared in the doorway. Cash tried to see Asa McCall through Molly's eyes. A large, still solid man, his blond hair graying at the temples, his eyes a blue much like Cash's. There was strength of character in his weathered face and in his ramrod-straight posture.

Cash had always respected his father. Not that he wasn't acutely aware of his faults.

"This is my father, Asa McCall," he said, feeling a sense of pride that surprised him.

Molly stepped forward, her hand outstretched. "Please call me Molly. It's an honor to meet you, sir."

Asa seemed amused. "My pleasure."

Shelby appeared then. Clearly, she had intended to ignore Jasmine.

"It is so nice to see you again," Molly said extending her hand.

Shelby had no choice but to take it. Her expression seemed to change from cool indifference to a scowl. Cash promised himself he wouldn't leave here without finding out why his mother hated Jasmine so.

"I feel like we got off on the wrong foot," Molly was saying to Shelby. "I know I look like Jasmine but I don't feel like her. I have little knowledge of her. I'm finding out things about her though that are very disturbing. Especially her behavior before she disappeared."

Shelby's eyes narrowed at such frankness.

"If I'm Jasmine, I'm very sorry if I hurt your son," Molly said. "I can't imagine a woman who wouldn't appreciate everything about Cash. He's a wonderful man who deserves to be happy."

Shelby seemed to thaw right before his eyes. Cash had never seen anything like it.

"We're going for a ride around the ranch," he said into the uncomfortable silence. "We'll be back in plenty of time for dinner."

"I would like to help," Molly said. "I'm not used to being waited on." She blushed. "At least not during any of the life I can recall."

"Come into the kitchen when you return," Shelby said. "I'm sure I can find something for you to do."

Molly smiled. "I'll do that."

Cash quickly ushered her out of the house. It wasn't until they were headed for the horse barn, out of earshot of the house, that he looked over at her. "How did you do that?"

She seemed surprised. "What?"

"Shelby. My mother. You completely turned her around in there. How did you do that?"

Molly laughed. He could no longer remember how Jasmine laughed, no longer cared. More and more, this woman was becoming Molly to him. Jasmine would never have handled his mother like that. Jasmine would have gotten mad, done her I'm-superior-to-all-of-you-people routine and made an enemy of his mother for life.

Molly's laugh hung for a moment in the clear morning air. "I don't know what you're talking about," she said, head held high as she headed off across the field ahead of him.

He watched her for a moment, thinking he didn't know this woman but he wanted to.

Molly smiled when Cash caught up to her. He chuckled softly as he walked beside her, realizing how much he liked her. He found himself half hoping she wasn't Jasmine, even knowing that would mean he'd still be a suspect in Jasmine's murder.

MOLLY GLANCED OVER at the man beside her as they fell into a companionable silence. She refused to think about tomorrow. She would enjoy this day, enjoy Cash and take the memory with her.

"See that tree," Cash said. "I fell out of it when I was five and broke my leg. It was J.T.'s fault. He said I couldn't climb as high as he could."

"But you did," she said, smiling over at him.

He laughed. "Oh yeah."

The day was bright, the sky a clear, deep blue, the cool morning air filling her lungs, filling her with...happiness.

The word surprised her, but she realized she *was* happy, a word she wouldn't have used to describe most of her life.

Cash made her feel good. So did his family. She'd even made progress with his mother. She knew none of that should have mattered. She had to leave tonight. She would never see any of them again.

But for today, she'd let herself be happy. She'd enjoy being a part of his family. She was safe. She wouldn't think about tonight. Or tomorrow. For today, she wasn't running anywhere.

"I thought you might like to ride Baby," Cash said as

he pushed open the barn door and led her to one of the stalls.

The mare raised her head, blinked big brown eyes at Molly and came over to nudge her hand on the gate. Molly heard Cash's intake of air.

"She likes you," he said.

Molly rubbed the white star between Baby's ears, surprised by the connection she felt. She'd never had a pet as a kid. Not with her and Max moving all the time. Not as an adult for the same reason. The horse was spotted brown and white and reminded her of western movies she'd seen. "What is she?"

"A pinto."

"She's beautiful."

"She's yours. As long as you're here," he added and looked embarrassed.

No one had ever offered her something so wonderful and with such generosity. She felt tears spring to her eyes as she stared at him. "No one has ever given me…" Her voice broke. He'd meant this horse for Jasmine. Not for the first time, she wished she *was* Jasmine. To be loved by this man… "Cash, thank you. That's so…"

"Romantic?" He laughed softly and touched her cheek.

The truth was like a stone in her throat. "But I'm not—"

"I know, you're Molly." He smiled. "Baby's very gentle. I broke her myself. You ready to ride her?"

Molly nodded. She was touched that she would get to ride her because she knew Jasmine never would.

She stood back and watched him as he saddled Baby and another larger horse named Zeke. She liked watching Cash's hands, the way they touched the horses, the way they worked. She understood the calluses she'd seen on those hands, this rancher, cowboy sheriff.

They rode behind the ranch house through deep wild grass up into the stands of aspens, the leaves rustling in the morning breeze.

"You ride well," Cash commented.

She had ridden horses when Max had been involved with a traveling Wild West show for a while. She felt at ease on Baby, felt even more at ease with Cash.

She watched his face, saw a peace in his expression that she hadn't seen in the time she'd known him. This was his home. This land. She envied him the way she had never sought money or fame. She envied him this place that made him so content.

The air smelled of pine as they rode higher, until they were on a bench overlooking the ranch. Cash dismounted and lifted Molly from Baby. The sun burned down on them. She walked to the edge of the bluff and looked out across the land. McCall land. She felt a lump in her throat. What it must be like to have a connection to all of this, a history, a future. "It's so peaceful."

"I thought we could have lunch by the creek," Cash said as he took off his saddlebag and motioned toward an outcropping of rocks and trees.

She could hear water running as she neared the trees. As she wound her way through the huge boulders, she came upon a picturesque creek. The water pooled among the rocks before tumbling down the mountainside.

Molly stepped to a flat spot at the edge of one of the clear blue pools, the water gurgling around the smooth boulders. "It looks so inviting," she said, already reaching down to unlace her tennis shoes.

Cash spread the blanket he'd brought under a huge pine and set down the picnic lunch he'd packed. When he turned, the last thing he expected was to see her with her shoes and socks off and stepping into the creek.

"The water is deeper than it looks and the rocks are slip—"

He didn't get his warning out before she slid into the pool and disappeared beneath the water. Hell. Did she know how to swim? Did she even know if she knew how to swim?

He raced to the edge of the creek, ready to jump in, clothes, boots, hat and all, when her head burst out of the water in a shower of droplets.

She was laughing, the water droplets glistening around her in the sunlight, her green eyes dancing and that wonderful laugh of hers hanging in the air.

He rocked back, taken completely off guard by the rush of feelings at just the sight of her. She looked like a drowned rat and couldn't have been more beautiful, soaking wet and laughing in that blue-green pool of water.

She also couldn't have looked less like Jasmine.

He put out his hand to help her out. She took it, still laughing. "I only meant to get my feet wet."

He shook his head. "I thought I was going to have to dive in and save you."

She came out of the water and shook her blond head, sending spray into the air. Her hair was curly now, not straight like she'd been wearing it. It cupped her face, making her green eyes seem larger, definitely brighter. The makeup she'd applied that morning had washed off.

He noticed for the first time that she had a sprinkling of light freckles across her cheeks and nose.

"Boy was *that* refreshing," she said grinning at him.

He caught his breath as his eyes locked with hers. This woman wasn't Jasmine. The shock rattled through him. He didn't need fingerprint results. He knew, soul deep. He grabbed her, gripping her upper arms, turning her to face him.

Molly saw his expression change an instant before he grabbed her. He looked as if he were about to say something, but then his mouth dropped to hers.

It was so unexpected, her breath caught, her lips parted and she kissed him back.

The kiss didn't last half a minute before Cash pulled back.

"Cash, there is something I have to tell you," she blurted out. "I'm not—"

His mouth was on hers again, his kiss overpowering her senses. She resisted at first. He thought he was kissing Jasmine. Not her. She desperately wanted to tell him the truth. She wanted him to kiss *her*. Molly Kilpatrick. She wanted his desire to be for her. Not the ghost of Jasmine Wolfe.

But his mouth was hot and unrelenting and she gave in to it, passion sparking and catching fire between them. She circled his neck with her arms as he grabbed her waist and drew her against him, wet clothes and all. She felt his need in the kiss, in the strength of his hands pulling her closer, in the hardness of his body.

She wanted him. It didn't matter who he thought she was. He was kissing *her*. Wanted *her*.

He drew back to look into her eyes. His fingers trailed along the side of her cheek, dipping to the open neck of her shirt, across the lace of her bra, across one already hard nipple.

His large hands cupped her breasts, warm fingers teasing her nipples, sending shafts of heat to her center. She groaned as those hands explored her body, his touch setting fire to her chilled skin as he stripped her naked, tossing each piece into the boughs of the pine tree to dry.

He stared at her, caressing her body with his gaze, making her skin tingle and ache. She closed her eyes as he kissed her neck, then dropped lower, taking one aching nipple in his mouth. Heat shot to her center. She groaned, cradling his head in her hands.

"Cash, oh Cash."

He stopped.

She opened her eyes.

He seemed surprised and overpowered by that desire, as if he hadn't expected this. Knew it was the last thing he should be doing with her. "Say you want me as much as I do you," he said, his voice breaking.

His words enflamed her. "I *want* you like I have never wanted anything in my life."

He dragged her to him with almost a sob as his mouth found hers again. They staggered over to the warm nest of pine needles where he'd spread the picnic blanket. And under the wide, sweeping, green branches of the tree, he stripped. She watched until there was nothing between them and he was on the blanket with her, his body as hot as her desire.

Their naked bodies glistened in the morning sun as they clung to each other with a passion like none Molly had ever dreamed.

Cash had never known anything like it. She was more beautiful naked than he could have imagined. She opened to him and he thought he would die if he didn't have her.

"I love your hands," she breathed against his mouth.

He cupped her breasts and looked into her eyes. Molly. She was Molly, the woman who loved food, laughed joyously, thought even the silliest of things were romantic. Molly.

At that moment it didn't matter why she'd come to Antelope Flats. Or who she'd called last night. Or why she was so afraid of the two men back in town.

Nothing mattered but her.

He kissed her, deepening the kiss as his hands touched her everywhere. He wanted to know her body as intimately as he knew her laugh. He wanted her, his desire so strong that nothing could stop it.

The cop in him told him he had no business making love to her. Even now that he knew she was Molly, he could still get his heart broken. Or worse. And what about her? What would she do once he told her he knew.

"Molly." He pulled back again to look at her. "Molly," he repeated.

She smiled, tears swimming in all that green.

He made love to her, the first time in a frenzy of need, the second time slowly, gently, lovingly on the blanket under the wide sweeping boughs of the pine tree, to the sound of the creek moving through the rocks.

She seemed to blossom under his fingers, her body a woman's, full and lush.

When they were both finally spent, they lay under the shade of the huge pine, the breeze stirring the branches over their heads, the soft whinny of the horses ground tied nearby, the gentle rise and fall of her breasts, her eyes closed, her lips turned up in a smile of contentment.

He smiled too as he pushed himself up on one elbow. Just looking at her filled him to overflowing. How had he lived without this woman?

How could he live without her when she left?

The thought startled him. Why would she leave?

Because she wasn't Jasmine.

He sat up abruptly and reached for his clothes.

She must have felt the movement. He heard her stir behind him.

"What is it?" she asked.

He didn't look at her. "It's getting late. We should get back."

She touched his shoulder and he turned to look at her. She'd pulled her blouse from a low pine bough and held it with one hand in front of herself as if to cover her beautiful breasts.

Just looking at her made him catch his breath again. She reached for him and the next thing he knew she was in his arms. He held her tight to him, wanting to make love to her again. And yet afraid of what he was feeling for her. A woman he couldn't trust. A woman he didn't know.

"Jasmine?" he breathed against her hair and felt her

tense. He'd called her Jasmine to remind himself of her lie. And remind her as well.

This time she was the one to draw back. "You're right. We should get back. I promised your mother I would help with dinner."

He dressed, his back to her, pretending to give her some privacy, when in truth he knew he would take her in his arms again if he looked at her and confessed that he knew she wasn't Jasmine. His desire for this woman was boundless. Inexhaustible.

But now more than ever he needed to know who she was. Who he was falling in love with.

Chapter Twelve

They rode back to the ranch, saying little. The air felt hot and close, and Molly was glad to get off the horse in the cool barn.

"Go on in. I can take care of this," Cash said without looking at her.

She stared at his broad back, wanting to touch him, wanting to say something. But telling him the truth now seemed the worst thing she could do. *Get through this family dinner. Then leave the first chance Cash gives you tonight. A clean break. No harm done.*

But even as she thought it, her heart broke at the thought of never seeing him again. No harm done, like hell. But she reminded herself that it wasn't her he'd made love to, but Jasmine.

You were so good at pretending you were Jasmine that you fell in love with her fiancée. But if he knew who you really were...

She entered the cool, elegant ranch house and stood for moment. Earlier she had wanted to be a part of this family so badly and had felt it for those few minutes.

But she didn't belong here. She never had. Jasmine would have fit in, Jasmine with her wealth, her privileged upbringing.

"There you are."

Molly turned to see Cash's mother.

"Is everything all right?" Shelby asked.

Molly nodded quickly and smiled. "Wonderful. The ride was…amazing. It just got hot out there." She couldn't help but look sheepish. "I fell in the creek."

"I like your hair better that way," Shelby said. "It suits you."

Molly wiped at her forehead, fighting back tears at the memory of being in Cash's arms under the sweeping pine.

"Freshen up in the bath down the hall, then come into the kitchen," Shelby offered. "I'll pour you a large glass of lemonade. You look like you could use it."

In the bathroom, Molly washed up, the cool water feeling good on her flushed, sweaty skin, the same way Cash's hands had felt hot on her cold skin. She touched the scar on her forehead. She'd told Cash the truth. She didn't know how she'd gotten it. The scar had just been there for as far back as she could remember. Max had said he didn't know when she'd gotten it or how. She knew he had to be lying. Wouldn't it have bled horribly?

She shut off the water. She could still smell Cash on her skin, still feel his touch. She closed her eyes trying not to cry. Then, getting control, she headed down the hall to find the large functional kitchen.

Shelby smiled when Molly came in, then handed her the promised glass of lemonade. The glass was cold and wet. She put it against her forehead for a moment, then took a sip of the lemonade inside.

"Thank you. It's delicious." She looked around. "What can I do?"

Shelby seemed to study her, then nodded. "Would you like to make the salad?"

"I would love to," Molly said with relief. She needed to keep busy. She needed not to think about Cash. Or the lie that had put her in this unbearable position.

CASH COULDN'T BELIEVE his family that night at dinner. Everyone was there, Rourke and Cassidy with news of their honeymoon—and the construction of their new house up the road in a corner of the ranch; J.T. and Reggie and their upcoming wedding plans, as well as the construction of their home; even Brandon and Dusty seemed in good spirits.

Cash looked around the table at his ever-growing family and felt a sense of pride in them tonight. He caught Asa and Shelby exchanging what could only be called intimate looks. They loved each other. There was no doubt about that.

"How was your horseback ride?" Reggie asked Molly.

"Reggie's been taking lessons," J.T. added. "Hasn't been bucked off in what? Hours?"

Everyone laughed, even Reggie. "You wait. I'm going to be a ranchwoman yet. You'll see."

"Even if it kills you," J.T. said, but with obvious pride.

"So how was your ride?" Reggie asked Molly again.

Molly had been avoiding looking at Cash during dinner. Not that he could blame her. He'd wanted to distance himself from her and calling her Jasmine up on the mountain had definitely done it. He swore at his own foolishness. He'd made love to Molly. Not Jasmine.

Now she glanced over at him as she answered. "The ride was wonderful. Everything about it was incredible. I've never experienced anything like it."

The room was suddenly silent as he locked eyes with her, sparks arcing between them. Then she seemed to sense the quiet and added hurriedly, looking down at her plate, "The ranch is so beautiful."

Cash saw the exchange of knowing smiles around the table and hoped to hell his face wasn't as red as Molly's.

"So when will your house be done?" he asked Rourke, trying to change the subject. But he could feel his mother's eyes on him. She hadn't missed the exchange between him and Molly.

The rest of the meal passed without incident. Just as the family housekeeper and cook Martha was about to serve dessert, the phone rang. Martha answered it and announced it was for Cash.

"I need to take this," he said rising. "I'm sorry. If you'll excuse me." He headed for his father's office and closed the door, knowing it was the call he'd been waiting for.

"Cash?" said the voice on the other end of the line. "It's Frank. Sorry I couldn't get back to you any sooner."

Cash had sent an e-mail to Frank with the fingerprints saying it was urgent he get the results. Frank had e-mailed right back while Molly had been cleaning the ink from her fingers to say he could have them in twenty-four hours.

"You said you needed these ASAP," Frank said.

"You have no idea. I can't thank you enough."

Frank sighed. "I hate to disappoint you, but they don't match Jasmine Wolfe's. But there is something interesting—"

"You're sure?" Cash interrupted, hearing only that Molly Kilpatrick's prints didn't match Jasmine's. She wasn't Jasmine. He'd known, of course, but now it was confirmed. He felt a swell of relief, then a deep sense of regret. Jasmine was likely dead. But he'd known that, too, hadn't he?

So who was Molly? She looked so much like Jasmine. When she wanted to, he realized. Molly was nothing like her. Especially now, after her dip in the creek, without makeup, her short blond locks curly, her face flushed from the sun. She looked very different from the woman who had come into his office the evening before.

With a jolt, he remembered how she'd rolled down the window in his pickup. Jasmine would never have done that because of her allergies. He swore. Jasmine might have changed over seven years, but she couldn't have overcome her allergies.

He should have seen it earlier, felt it the moment he touched her, let alone kissed her.

"Definitely no match but as I was saying, the interesting thing is that the prints you sent me did come up in another matter."

Frank's words finally registered. "You have Molly Kilpatrick's prints on file?" Cash sat down hard at his father's desk, his heart in his throat. That meant she was wanted for something.

"Not on file, but a red flag came up on them. I'm going to have to track 'em down," Frank said. "I'll call you as soon as I have something. Meanwhile, you want me to fax what I have to your office?"

"Could you fax it here?" He gave Frank his father's fax number there at the ranch, then hung up and waited for the report.

He thought about when he was taking Molly's prints. She hadn't known hers were on file or she would never have agreed to it. What the hell was she wanted for? He shuddered to think.

One thing was clear: she had to know she wasn't Jasmine Wolfe. So who was she?

And maybe more important, why was she pretending to be Jasmine?

Archie Wolfe's fortune? What else? But how did she hope to pull that off once her fingerprints didn't match Jasmine's? Did she hope to get money out of Bernard before the print results came back?

Good luck with that.

Cash scrubbed a hand over his face as the report rolled out of the fax machine, his dread growing. He couldn't let on that he knew she wasn't Jasmine. Which might work out, since he needed her to be Jasmine. Desperately needed her to be alive—until he could find out who killed her. Until he could clear his name.

As he was folding the fax, he heard the door open behind him and turned, expecting it would be Molly. His mother came in, closing the door firmly behind her.

Oh boy. He knew what was coming. If he'd learned anything about his mother since she'd come back from the dead, it was how perceptive she was. He'd seen her watching them all, learning things they thought they kept hidden. Hidden from most people anyway.

"If this is about Molly—"

"Of course it's about Molly," his mother snapped. "I'm worried about you."

"Didn't we already have this discussion last night? I told you I know what I'm doing."

She made a face as if she knew better. "You've fallen in love with this woman."

"That is old news. I think you know I was engaged to Jasmine seven years ago."

"No, not Jasmine," Shelby said with obvious irritation. "Molly. You're in love with Molly."

He stared at his mother. Did she know that Molly wasn't Jasmine? Given the way she'd treated Molly last night compared to tonight… "You lost me."

"I really doubt that," she said. "This woman isn't the woman you knew seven years ago."

No kidding.

"Stop looking for that woman and appreciate what's right in front of your eyes," she said, sounding angry.

He laughed. "Whoa, wait a minute. Last night you told me not to trust her."

"Last night I thought she was Jasmine."

He stared at his mother.

"Don't give me that look. Jasmine hurt you. Get over it. This woman isn't Jasmine. She's…Molly."

His mother meant well but she had no idea what she was talking about.

"We're all waiting on you before we have dessert," Shelby said and turned on her heel and left the room.

"Oh, she's Molly all right, but who the hell is Molly?" he said to himself as he followed her back toward the dining room, stopping to stuff the fax into the pocket of his jacket hanging in the hallway.

MOLLY WONDERED what important phone call Cash had gone to answer and why it was taking him so long. She tried not to watch the door, tried not to look anxious for his return.

Had Jasmine's body been found? Or Jasmine herself?

Right now, it would have been a relief to have this all end. She needed to leave one way or the other. Earlier, she'd tried to tell Cash the truth but he hadn't wanted to hear it. He wanted her to be Jasmine. Not Molly Kilpatrick.

A few minutes ago, Cash's mother had excused herself and disappeared down the hall, obviously going to check on him. Molly had wanted to go as well. As time passed, she felt herself growing more anxious.

She looked up. Shelby came back into the room. Cash wasn't far behind. He didn't meet her eyes as he sat back down.

"I'm sorry. It was official business," he said.

"Is everything all right?" his father asked.

Cash took a bite of his dessert as if stalling for time. He was different. And it wasn't her imagination. She'd been trained to read people. Cash was upset, shaken. What had the phone call been about?

"The bartender at the Mello Dee was killed last

night," Cash said after a moment. "Teresa Clark." He glanced at his youngest brother Brandon. "You haven't been going out there have you?"

Brandon shook his head. "I thought the place was closed."

"Was she murdered?" Dusty asked.

"Can we please talk of more pleasant things?" Shelby interrupted. "Cassidy, didn't you have something you wanted to say?"

Everyone looked down the table at Cassidy. She blushed then nodded as she reached for her husband's hand. "Rourke and I are expecting!"

There were cheers and applause. Molly found herself in tears and hurriedly wiped at them, offering her congratulations. Cassidy looked so happy and Rourke, who looked like all the McCall men—blond, blue-eyed and handsome—beamed.

Of course none of the McCall boys was as handsome as Cash, Molly thought as the meal wound down and Cash announced that they had to leave. "I need to pick up those cinnamon rolls you have for me," he said to Cassidy.

"I left them at your office. I thought that would be handier for you," Cassidy said.

Molly watched the exchange. Cash was picking up more cinnamon rolls? How odd, she thought, remembering how he'd had to stop by the café before they came out to the ranch. If it was just to order more cinnamon rolls, he could have called or waited to see her once they got to the ranch.

Molly didn't want to leave here and go back to town.

She'd felt so safe on the ranch with Cash and his family that she'd put Vince and Angel out of her mind for a while. The men would be looking for her back in town. Could be waiting for her in the shadows around Cash's house. She couldn't jeopardize his life by not warning him.

To her surprise, Shelby hugged her as they were leaving. Molly saw Cash's surprise—and the frown when Dusty also hugged her. He didn't want her getting any closer to his family, she realized. Why was that?

Did he regret their lovemaking? Or was he just keeping her at arm's length until he knew who she was, afraid of getting involved with a woman who might be…say, the daughter of a known criminal, she thought ruefully.

Cash said little as they left the ranch. She debated what to tell him. His silence scared her.

"I need to tell you something," she said as they neared town. She had to tell him the truth. She had to warn him about Vince and Angel.

"Can it wait?" he asked as he pulled up in front of the sheriff's office. "I just need to run in here for a minute, then we can go back to the house. We can talk there, all right?"

He didn't give her a chance to argue. He hopped out of the pickup. She watched him unlock his office and step inside, the light coming on behind the blinds.

ONCE INSIDE HIS OFFICE, Cash sat down at the computer and typed in a description of the men, suspecting there might be a warrant out on them since Molly's prints had come up on the FBI's radar.

Still, he was surprised when he got a hit. There was an APB out on two men matching their descriptions. Their names were Vince Winslow and Angel Edwards, and both were wanted for questioning by the Las Vegas Police Department in the murder of a man named Lanny Giliano.

"Lanny?" That was the name of the man Molly had called last night. Cash put his head in his hands. What the hell was Molly mixed up in?

There was no reason to run the prints of the two men. Vince Winslow and Angel Edwards were in Antelope Flats. Nor did it take much to figure out why. They were here because of Molly.

He picked up the phone and called the Las Vegas Police Department, got the detective in the Lanny Giliano case on the line and told him he'd seen Vince and Angel.

As the detective filled him in, Cash stared out through the blinds at his pickup and Molly. He could see her dark silhouette in the front seat.

A few minutes later, he hung up, opened his desk drawer and took out his gun. Officially, he'd been relieved of duty by Mathews. He'd have to work around that small problem. As he strapped on the gun, he thought about the chilling news the Vegas homicide detective had given him.

Vince and Angel were dangerous monsters who'd mutilated a man in Vegas before they killed him. Lanny Giliano. A man who'd been in on a diamond heist with them fifteen years ago.

The same man Molly had tried to call last night from the phone in Cash's den.

He sat for a moment, stunned by what he'd learned. As he started to rise from his desk, he saw that he'd gotten a message while he was on the line with the detective. He hurriedly retrieved it.

"This is Greg at the Dew Drop Inn near Bozeman? You left me a message? I had to go through my records but I can tell you who was working the night you asked about seven years ago." The man sounded pleased that he kept such good accounts. Not half as pleased as Cash.

The guy cleared his throat and continued. "The bartender on duty that night was Teresa Clark. Everyone called her T.C. Last I heard she was out in Seattle. Hope that helps you." The message ended.

Teresa Clark. The woman who was murdered at the Mello Dee.

He picked up the phone and called State Investigator John Mathews.

MOLLY SLID DOWN IN THE SEAT a little. Main Street was empty. No cars cruised by. But still she cracked her window so she could hear if anyone approached the truck on foot. She wished Cash would hurry. She watched the light in his office, could see his shadow moving around inside. She was anxious for him to return, anxious to end this.

"Why won't you let me tell you the truth?" she asked, staring at his shadow through the blinds.

She knew now that she couldn't just leave tonight without telling him about Vince and Angel. She couldn't leave him here without knowing that he was in danger. She had led Vince and Angel here. They could find out that she'd been staying with the sheriff. They would think he knew where she was.

She shuddered as she imagined what they might do to him. Whether Cash wanted to hear it or not, she was going to tell him everything.

She hated to think how he would take finding out that she wasn't Jasmine, wasn't the woman he'd loved and lost, especially after their lovemaking today.

She watched the street, her anxiety growing. *Hurry up, Cash.* If he didn't come out soon, she was going in. He would listen to her. She would make him.

She shivered and looked over, noticing Cash's jean jacket on the seat between them. She picked it up. He wouldn't mind if she put it on. One of the pockets bulged. She remembered him in the jacket earlier that morning on the ride. The pockets had been empty then.

Curious, she pulled the folded paper out. Did this have something to do with the urgent call he'd received during dinner about the murder at the Mello Dee?

She saw at once that the sheet was a fax and, even in the faint light coming through the blinds of his office, she could read the words *FBI* and *fingerprints*. Her heart stopped. Cash had gotten the results. That's what the phone call had been. He'd said it would take at least a week. Maybe two. He'd lied to her?

He knew she wasn't Jasmine! When was he going to tell her? And what would he do now?

She didn't need to read the report. She knew she wasn't Jasmine Wolfe and that her fingerprints wouldn't match. She started to refold the fax, not realizing Cash had come out of his office.

She looked up. He was standing at the driver's side window looking in at her. Her heart stopped. He opened the door and she saw that he had a small box of cinnamon rolls in his hands and was wearing a gun.

Chapter Thirteen

Cash looked from her to the fax in her hand.

"Why haven't you said anything?" Her voice came out a whisper.

He took the report from her hand, angry with himself for leaving it in the truck. Had he wanted her to find it? "Did you read it?"

"I didn't have to," she said. "I tried to tell you earlier. You stopped me."

He looked over at her as he put the key into the ignition and started the pickup. "I didn't want to hear that you weren't Jasmine." He saw the effect his words had on her and wished he could rein them back in. "I'm sorry, what I meant was—"

"You don't have to apologize. I know how badly you wanted me to be Jasmine," she said. "I'm sorry I disappointed you. I can see how much you loved her, how much you wanted her back."

He shut off the engine and raked a hand through his hair. "Look, I know about Vince Winslow and Angel Edwards. I know you tried to call Lanny Giliano last night from my phone in the den. I know about the Hollywood diamond heist fifteen years ago with another man, Max Burke. Max got killed. Vince and Angel got fifteen years. They just got out. I know Lanny is dead—"

"He's dead?"

"Sorry," he said seeing her eyes well with tears.

"I knew he was dead. I was just hoping…"

"Why are Vince and Angel in town?"

"They're looking for me. They plan to kill me—after I tell them where the diamonds are from the heist. They think I know."

"Why would you know?"

"My father was the third man in the heist, Max Burke, better known as the Great Maximilian Burke, magician and thief."

"Do you have the diamonds?"

She shook her head. "I don't have any idea where they are, but Vince and Angel won't believe that. My father had the diamonds after the heist. I was the last person to see him alive. But he didn't live long enough to tell me what he did with them. Vince saw Max say something to me but it had nothing to do with the diamonds. All Max said was, 'I'm sorry, kiddo. I'll try to make it up to you.' Then he died."

"I'm sorry."

Molly looked over at him. "My father was shot down by police in the street when he tried to get away. He died in my arms. I was fourteen." She looked away, but nothing could hide the pain. "I'm the daughter of a thief. Now you know."

How could he have ever thought she was Jasmine?

This woman felt so much, so deeply. "That must have been horrible for you. What about your mother?"

"She died when I was a baby."

"What did you do after your father died?"

"I ran." She looked over at him. "That's what I've been doing the past fifteen years—running. I knew Vince and Angel could get out at any time. That's what I was doing when I came here, running from them. When I saw the photograph and story in the newspaper about Jasmine and saw the resemblance… I needed a place to hide for a while until Vince and Angel were picked up. I knew they murdered Lanny even though the police wouldn't tell me anything when I called." Her eyes filled with tears. She wiped at them, biting her lower lip in a way that he knew Jasmine never had. "I hated lying to you."

"We've both been lying to each other," he said and pulled her into his arms, holding her tightly. Her story matched what the Las Vegas police had told him. He would have believed her even if it hadn't. Whatever reason her prints came up on the FBI's system, it must have something to do with her father. He pushed it out of his mind. All that mattered was keeping her safe. For the moment.

"Let's talk about this at home," he said. Home. He'd actually called that rambling old house home?

"No," she said, grabbing his arm. "Vince and Angel could be there. You don't know these men. They wouldn't hesitate to kill you."

He smiled. "I called Mathews. He's got highway patrol looking for them right now." She was worried about

getting *him* killed now? "Vince and Angel aren't waiting for us. This morning when I fixed your car so you
couldn't leave I found a global positioning device on it."

"That's how they found me? I didn't think they were
that smart."

"Prison is a great crime school."

Her eyes widened. "They could have killed me in
Vegas. Why track me?"

"They must have thought you would lead them to the
diamonds."

"Instead, I led them to you," she said, tears in her eyes
as she looked over at him.

"I put the GPS on a coal car heading south and sent
Vince and Angel on a wild-goose chase until I could find
out why you were so afraid of them. I couldn't help but
notice your reaction when you saw them."

"They'll be back," she said, looking afraid. "Only
now they'll be even more angry and they'll come to the
last place they tracked me. You." She groaned. "You
shouldn't have done that. You don't know what these
men are capable of."

"You don't know what I'm capable of," he said.
"There's an APB out on them. They'll get picked up."

She looked skeptical.

"Or I'll deal with them." He drove toward the house.
"I want you to get your things. I'm taking you to the
family lake cabin. Vince and Angel won't be able to find
you there."

"You know they'll come back to the house, that's why
you want to get rid of me. You think you'll lay a trap for
them. Well I'm not leaving you alone to face them."

He glanced over at her, ready to more than argue the point, but he was distracted at the sight of an SUV parked in front of his house. A rental. He parked behind it with a curse. "Stay here."

As he stepped out of the pickup, he heard the squeak of the porch swing. Bernard Wolfe was sprawled on it as if he'd been waiting for some time. Behind him, Cash heard Molly open her door and get out.

Cash swore under his breath. He had to get Molly out of town and right away.

"I WANT TO TALK TO MY SISTER alone," Bernard said, getting to his feet and coming across the porch to meet them.

Cash started to tell him it would be a cold day in hell before that happened.

"Could you leave us alone?" Molly asked. "Please. I really do need to talk to my stepbrother."

Cash saw Bernard's jaw tighten at the word *stepbrother*. Cash looked over at Molly. He wasn't leaving her alone with Bernard. What the hell was she thinking?

"Please," she said. "Bernard looks like he could use a drink. You don't mind if I show him to your bar, do you?"

Hell yes, he minded and she knew it. What was she up to? Whatever it was, he didn't like it. But he also couldn't keep her from talking to Bernard, short of locking her up in his jail. Even then, he figured Bernard would spring her.

"I'll be right here if you need me," Cash said, crossing his arms, feet planted on the porch. "Make it quick."

MOLLY OPENED THE DOOR to the house, amazed Cash still hadn't bothered to lock it when they'd left. She hoped Vince and Angel hadn't gotten wise to the wild-goose chase and doubled back already. She worried that Cash would underestimate Vince and Angel. It would be his last mistake.

She stepped inside, turning on the lights as she led Bernard to the living room.

All the color had drained from his face. "Jasmine. It really is you."

She didn't correct him. Something about his demeanor put her on guard even though she couldn't believe he would try to hurt her, not with Cash right outside the door.

"When Kerrington told me you were alive…" He shook his head as if he still couldn't believe it. "I really could use that drink."

She motioned toward the bar. As Bernard poured himself a drink, she noticed that his hands were shaking. She declined when he offered to make her one as well.

He was visibly nervous. She watched him look around the room, then at her. "Kerrington says you have amnesia."

"You seem nervous, Bernard," she said mimicking Jasmine's voice. "Are you worried that I'm going to remember what happened the day I disappeared?"

He froze. "You remember?"

Molly thought about the woman whose life she'd stepped into. Didn't she owe Jasmine? Karma-wise no doubt about it. But the truth was, Molly couldn't walk away and let Cash continue living under this veil of suspicion. She owed him. If she could find out what happened to the woman he'd loved, she had to try. And as long as the people who'd been closest to her still thought she was Jasmine…

"You didn't want me marrying the sheriff," she said.

"You weren't going to marry him," Bernard said scowling at her as he took a drink.

"I loved him."

Bernard's laugh cut her to the quick. "You made fun of the fool with me and Kerrington. Maybe you really don't remember, but the three of us used to go to that bar where you and Kerrington hung out all the time. You would tell stories about your cowboy. Hell, you were sleeping with Kerrington. The only reason you said you were engaged to the sheriff was to piss off your father. And drive Kerrington crazy. If the sheriff found out what you were really up to…"

"Someone tried to kill me."

"Like I said. If your sheriff found out what you were really up to…"

"Cash didn't try to kill me."

"Well, don't look at me."

"You had the most to gain. You stood to inherit everything with me out of the way."

He took another sip of his drink. "I'll admit I haven't missed you. All those years of trying to keep you out of trouble. But you're barking up the wrong tree if you think I was the one who did this to you." His laugh was self-deprecating. "Hell, Jazz, I was half in love with you myself. But I'm sure you know that."

Her shock must have shown.

"Or maybe not. Even though we weren't related by

blood, you never thought of me as anything more than a brother." He sounded bitter. "You ridiculed me behind my back as badly as you did everyone else, didn't you?" He nodded. "I suspected as much. But that's all water under the bridge since you don't remember it," he said sarcastically.

"I'm sorry," Jasmine had obviously hurt him badly. And not just him. Kerrington, too. Sandra and Patty. And Cash?

"Sorry?" Bernard said, as if he'd never heard the word come out of Jasmine's mouth. "You're sorry?" He drained his glass and put it down a little too hard on the bar. "What are you sorry for, Jazz? Sorry that you hurt people? Or sorry that for seven years we've been free of you and your games?"

She held her ground. He was inches from her now, his dark eyes hateful.

"Or are you sorry that one of us finally had enough and tried to kill you?" he asked, his voice hoarse with emotion. "Any one of us wanted you dead at one point or another. Kerrington. Sandra. Patty. Me. I just never had the stomach for murder."

"Really?" She played the card up her sleeve. "My memory is starting to come back, Bernard. It's just a matter of time before I know which one of you did it."

His face went ashen, his breath coming hard. "It wasn't me. I'll give you half of everything. But if you try to take it all by trying to frame me, I warn you I'll—"

"What will you do?" Cash asked from the doorway.

Bernard swung around in obvious surprise, as if he'd forgotten about Cash. "Just a little family matter,"

Bernard said and gave Molly a knowing look as he brushed past her and left.

Molly realized she was trembling uncontrollably. She'd thought by telling him that she remembered the day she disappeared, he would be frightened. Instead, he was furious, thinking she would try to frame him?

"What the hell are you trying to do?" Cash grabbed her by her upper arms. "Get yourself killed?"

She was too shocked to speak. She'd never heard him raise his voice, let alone seen him this furious. His fingers were biting into her flesh.

Bernard's words rang in her ears. *If your sheriff had found out what you were really up to...*

Cash saw the fear in her eyes and quickly let go. "I'm sorry. But do you realize what you've done, telling Bernard that your memory is coming back?" He swore. Just the sight of her reminded him of their lovemaking up on the mountain overlooking the ranch. He was angry with her for lying to him, but at the same time he wanted to pull her into his arms and make love to her all over again. "Aren't you in enough danger? Molly, why in the hell would you do that?"

"I owe it to Jasmine for stealing her life."

"What are you talking about?" he demanded. "You don't owe Jasmine anything." He caught one of her short blond curls between his fingers. "You're more beautiful than she was in so many ways."

"I owe it to you," she said, sounding close to tears.

He let go of her hair. He wanted to shake some sense into her. "Me?"

His face was stone. In it, Molly saw nothing of the

man who'd made passionate love to her earlier on the mountain. She feared she might never see that man again.

"I'm sorry, Cash. When I came up with this plan, I hadn't met you, I never thought…" Never thought that she might fall in love with the sheriff of Antelope Flats. Isn't that what she was going to say? "I'm sorry. I didn't mean to hurt you."

"Hurt me? You think that's what I care about? You're nothing like Jasmine. I should have known right away and put a stop to this."

She felt as if he'd slapped her. "I know how much you loved her…." She turned away, unable to face him and say the words. "Let me help you find her killer—"

He spun her around to face him. "Listen to me. She wasn't the love of my life. I won't have you lose *your* life for something that wasn't true."

She stared at him. "You were engaged to be married."

He raked a hand through his hair and shook his head.

Fear squeezed her heart like a fist. He'd been keeping something from her about him and Jasmine. She'd known it. "Tell me," she said, her voice a whisper.

He shook his head again, but she'd already seen the answer in his face.

"You knew," she said on a breath. "You knew about her and Kerrington."

He didn't move, didn't speak, his face frozen in a mask of ice.

Her body went cold. "I know you didn't kill her," she said, fear compressing her lungs, making it hard to catch her breath. But she also knew he'd done something,

something he'd been hiding. "I know there's something you aren't telling me."

His face seemed to melt, his expression going from anger to pain. He slumped, turning away from her.

She reached out, touched his shoulder, felt the warmth of his body beneath her fingers. She wanted to wrap her arms around him and tell him everything was going to be all right, but she feared that was a lie.

He turned slowly to look at her. "I *wanted* to kill her."

"But you didn't. You couldn't."

His smile held no humor. "How can you be so sure of that?"

She shook her head. She didn't know how, just that her heart promised her it was true. "You aren't a killer."

He looked down at the floor, then up at her. "Jasmine and I were *never* engaged. She told everyone we were. I went up to Bozeman the day before she disappeared to find out why she'd done that. Jasmine and I dated a couple of times. I was flattered. Jasmine had a way of making you feel like you were the most important thing in her life." He sighed.

"You found her with Kerrington," Molly guessed.

He nodded. "They didn't see me."

Molly held her breath.

"I waited until she was alone." He raked his fingers through his hair. "It got ugly. She admitted that she was just using me in some game she had going with Kerrington and her father. I demanded she call off the newspapers who'd been hounding me about this stupid engagement. I had avoided the press, not wanting to embarrass Jasmine. I wanted her to call them back and tell them we weren't engaged."

He walked over to the front window, his back to her. "I found out that she'd even gotten a key to the house I'd just bought and was telling everyone it was my engagement present to her. I demanded it back. She jumped into her new little red sports car and took off. I run my pickup into her car, denting the side, taking out a headlight."

Molly couldn't help her startled expression. There would be evidence of an accident on Jasmine's car.

"I was sorry at once and offered to have it fixed. She was livid. Damaging her car was the ultimate sin. If she had had a weapon, she would have shot me on the spot. I know I should have told the state investigators as soon as I heard Jasmine was missing…"

So that's what he'd been hiding.

"I thought it was a stunt, her being missing. That she *wanted* me to look guilty, that she was trying to take away the one thing that meant anything to me, being a sheriff. The accident had happened the day before she disappeared. It didn't seem relevant. Then, once it appeared she really was missing, it was too late." He raked a hand through his hair again as he turned to look at her. "I kept waiting for her to turn up. I refused to believe she was dead. Then when you walked into my office…"

"I'm sorry."

"I can't tell you how much I hoped you were Jasmine," he said. He must have seen her change of expression. "Not because I loved Jasmine but if she was alive, then I was off the hook."

"You believe she's dead?" Molly asked.

"If Jasmine was alive, she wouldn't have waited seven years to come back and seek her revenge."

"What does she have to be vengeful about?"

"Jasmine didn't need a reason. Her father had just disinherited her. She was angry." He shook his head. "The irony is, after she disappeared Archie and I finally met. He liked me, said he would have been proud to have me for a son-in-law, thought I would be good for his daughter. It was Kerrington he didn't want her marrying. And Archie would never have left Jasmine penniless no matter what she did. It was just this battle between the two of them. He left part of his estate to Jasmine always holding out hope that she was still alive. Another reason Bernard must be beside himself thinking you're Jasmine."

"Why do you think she was driving down to Antelope Flats?"

"It wasn't to fix things up with me, I can tell you that. Maybe she wasn't driving down here at all. Whoever hid her car in that barn might have done it to frame me for her murder."

"Jasmine seems to have had a few enemies," Molly said.

He laughed. "That's putting it mildly. That's why we have to let them know that you aren't Jasmine. If I'm right, one of them killed her, possibly left her for dead. That person can't let Jasmine remember what happened that day." She shivered and he pulled her to him. "The sooner we make the announcement the better."

She smiled up at him. He was so trusting. Deception

came hard to him and because of that he would never understand the world she came from. "Cash, her killer is just going to think you're trying to protect me until I remember and you can arrest him. We have Jasmine's killer right where we want him. If we work this together—"

He started to argue but she put a finger to his lips.

"It's too late to do anything else and you know it." She met his pale blue eyes and felt a jolt. His look sent heat straight to her center, making her ache for him. His mouth dropped to hers in a kiss that curled her toes.

Sweeping her up into his arms, he headed for the stairs. "Don't you want to hear my plan?" she asked.

"No," he said. "I want to make love to you."

The doorbell rang. He ignored it and started up the steps. The doorbell rang again and a deep voice said, "It's Mathews. Open up."

Chapter Fourteen

With obvious reluctance, Cash set Molly down on her feet with a curse as Mathews pounded on the door.

"Sounds like I'd better tell you my plan quickly," Molly said.

"Just a minute!" Cash called to Mathews and Molly told him her plan.

Cash swore again and went to open the door. "Come on in," he said to a steaming John Mathews.

"What took you so long?" Mathews demanded, then saw Molly and stopped dead in his tracks. "Jasmine? What the hell, Cash?"

"Come on in. Wanna drink?" Cash asked.

"Am I going to need one?" Mathews asked.

"It might not hurt. State Lead Investigator John Mathews meet Molly Kilpatrick."

Mathews frowned, his gaze going from Molly to Cash and back again. "Not Jasmine Wolfe?"

"No, I just look like her," Molly said, holding out her hand.

He shook it. "Cash, I thought I told you to stay away

from this investigation. In fact, I relieved you of your duties as I recall."

"Look, John—"

"I want to help you catch Jasmine's killer," Molly interjected. "I've already started the ball rolling, so to speak."

"I think I will take that drink," Mathews said.

Cash led him into the living room. Molly perched on the edge of one of the chairs. Mathews lowered his large frame into a chair opposite her as Cash made them all drinks.

"I came over because of the Teresa Clark murder," Mathews said, taking the drink Cash offered him.

When Cash had called him from his office, he'd told Mathews what he'd learned about the bartender and the matchbook found in Jasmine's car.

"I thought you'd like to know that Teresa Clark talked to one of her regulars here in Antelope Flats, Charley Alberta, before she was killed. She said she knew the woman who's car was found. And that the last time she saw Jasmine Wolfe was the night Jasmine disappeared seven years ago. It seemed Jasmine came into the Dew Drop Inn all the time with two different men. Based on her descriptions of the men according to Charley, one was her brother Bernard. The other was Kerrington. It seems Bernard had a fight with Jasmine the night she disappeared and he left the bar. Then Kerrington came in and got into it with her, even following her outside, still arguing."

"On the day Bernard and Kerrington both said they were hiking and camping in the backcountry together?" Cash asked.

Mathews nodded. "Teresa Clark could have blown apart both of their alibis. Had she lived. Guess who had a drink at the Mello Dee the night Teresa Clark was murdered? Kerrington, only he lied and said he didn't know her, even gave her a fake name."

"Kerrington," Cash said like a curse.

Mathews nodded. "I came by to tell you before I go pick him up at the motel and to tell you that if you continue to butt into my case I'm going to throw your ass in jail."

"Then you probably aren't going to want to hear about the plan Molly came up with," Cash said. "But I think you should hear her out. As much as I don't like it, it's a damned good plan and it might put an end to this once and for all."

Mathews took a gulp of his drink and looked to Molly. "There's probably a good reason you look so much like Jasmine Wolfe."

"There is, but that's not important right now. I think I know how we can catch Jasmine's killer. By using me as bait."

"And you think this is a *good* idea?" Mathews said. "You got a death wish?"

HOW COULD MOLLY EXPLAIN that she'd fallen in love with Cash and wanted to help him? That she owed this to Jasmine because she'd stolen the woman's identity to save herself?

Cash filled Mathews in on how Molly had seen the story in the newspaper and noticed the remarkable resemblance.

Mathews raised one heavy brow. "And what did you hope to gain by pretending to be her? Jail time?"

"Time." Molly filled him in on Vince and Angel.

Mathews whistled and shook his head. "And that's when you got this harebrained idea that you could catch her killer?"

She nodded, ignoring the harebrained part. "By then I'd met Jasmine's former fiancée, Kerrington Landow, her stepbrother, Bernard, and her two former roommates, Sandra Perkins Landow and Patty Franklin. Anyone of them could have killed her."

"I agree on that account anyway," Mathews said.

"Today, I told them that I was starting to remember what happened the day I disappeared," Molly said. "The killer won't come after me—until he or she knows for certain that I'm Jasmine. There is only one way the killer can be sure of that. Dig up my grave."

Mathews drew back as if she'd hit him.

"But the killer can't check the grave because you have men out there looking for it yourself," Cash put in.

Mathews was nodding. "Let me guess. I pull off my men, stake out the farm, catch the killer."

"Pretty much," Cash said.

"Except you need to let the suspects know it is suspected that I'm Jasmine, that there is a chance my memory is returning and the search of the farm has been called off until the fingerprint results come back," Molly said.

Mathews shook his head. "You think the killer will go to her grave tonight to make sure she's there."

Cash nodded. "I think the only reason he hasn't gone

there already is that the farm has been crawling with investigators twenty-four-seven since her car was found."

"I suppose I could have my men stake out the farm—"

"No," Cash said. "We don't know which way the killer will access the farm. I know the area. I know a place where I can see most of the farm. And if your men don't leave, the killer will know in a town this size."

"Cash, if you think I'm letting you go alone—"

"You don't still think I'm the one who killed her?" Cash said in obvious frustration.

"I've never thought that. But I need to cover my behind—and yours. Don't forget, you've been relieved as sheriff."

Cash started to argue but Mathews cut him off. "You have a point though about the stakeout and you do know the property. You can go in with me. I'll deputize you."

"What about Molly?" Cash asked.

"I'll put three of my best men on the house," Mathews said.

"Wait a minute, don't I have some say in this?" Molly protested.

"No!" they both said in unison.

"It was my idea. I want to be there when the killer is arrested," she complained.

"Not a chance. You'll stay here in the house with guards right outside so I know you're safe until we get back," Cash said. "No argument. Otherwise John has the authority to lock you up in jail."

"That's not a bad idea," Mathews said. "I'm definitely going to want to ask you more about the two men after you and that little issue of identity fraud, so don't get leaving into your head."

"I'm not going anywhere," she said. "Not with three men guarding the house."

Cash looked as if he wished she had a half dozen or more guarding her.

"How soon can we do this?" Cash asked.

"I'll set everything in motion. I guess we're on for tonight. If I were the killer I'd want to find out just as quick as I could," Mathews said as he got to his feet. "I'll go let Bernard, Kerrington, Sandra and Patty know. They're all staying at the Lariat. On my way here, I noticed that they had all returned from dinner."

"You've had them under surveillance?" Cash asked in surprise.

"Isn't that what you would have done if you were still sheriff and not involved in this case?" Mathews said with a smile. "I just wish I had put a tail on them before Teresa Clark was killed."

Molly listened as Cash and John Mathews worked out the details. She couldn't help but be anxious. Cash was going out by the lake to trap a killer.

Mathews used Cash's phone in the den to make the call to the motel. She heard Cash in the kitchen, then upstairs. What was he doing? Searching the house, she thought. Making sure she was safe.

"Are you sure you'll be all right here by yourself?" he asked when he joined her in the living room.

"I won't be by myself," she reminded him. "It's you I'm worried about. She cupped his warm cheek in her hand. His face was rough with stubble. He had never looked more handsome. "Be careful?"

He smiled and nodded.

Mathews came back into the room. "It's all set. My men are here. I'll have them stay outside out of sight."

"Lock the door behind me," Cash said to her. "Don't let anyone in, no matter what."

"Don't worry. I'll be fine. There's still brownies in the cupboard, right?"

He smiled, his gaze locking with hers, and for just a moment she thought he would tell her that he loved her. The daughter of a known crook? Not likely.

"Ready?" Mathews said behind him in the now-open doorway.

Cash nodded, pulling her to him and kissing her hard. "I'll be back as soon as I can." And then he was gone.

She waited until the sound of the car engine died away in the distance, still reeling from the kiss. Going to the door, she peered through the peephole. She couldn't see anyone. But then that was the way it was supposed to work.

Locking the door, she turned to look at the old house. It needed so much work. She'd been delighted to hear that he hadn't bought the house for Jasmine. It didn't sound like she was the kind of woman who would want to strip all this woodwork. Same with the hardwood floors.

Molly squinted, imagining the house with a fresh coat of paint, something bright and cheery for the kitchen and maybe a nice sage green for the living room. As for the foyer—

She stopped herself cold, surprised at her train of thought. She hated old houses. And it would take months if not years to remodel this one. She'd never stayed that long in any one place in her life.

She heard a creak upstairs and froze, waiting to hear it again. Nothing. Suspicious noise was the reason she'd never liked old houses. Right now she didn't like being alone in this one without Cash. Vince and Angel could break into this house way too easily. The men were professionals.

But her real worry was for Cash. She knew she wouldn't be able to sit still until he came back. Just let him be safe. Let him catch the killer. Let him finally be free of Jasmine. Let Vince and Angel be caught. Let this be over.

But then he will also be free of you.

Right.

She told herself he would be back soon. In the meantime what she needed was brownies. She started to go into the kitchen to find them when she heard another creak of a floorboard upstairs.

Could it be one of the cops Mathews left to protect her? Cash had searched the house and if she knew him, had double-checked to make sure all the doors and windows were locked.

Unless someone had been in the house and he'd missed them. After all, he had been looking for two men: Vince and Angel.

She listened and heard nothing. It was an old house. Old houses creaked and groaned. She was just being paranoid. Still, she waited. Not a sound.

Brownies. She needed brownies. And a glass of milk. Comfort food. She glanced at the clock and prayed Cash would be back soon. In only a few days everything had changed for her. Where she had once always loved the idea of not knowing where she was going or what she would do when she got there, that life now had little appeal.

She didn't feel the need to hit the road. In fact, dreaded the thought of leaving here. Leaving Cash.

What would he do when she was gone? Start over. Just as she would have to do.

She wandered into the kitchen, not surprised to find the brownies on the counter, covered in plastic with a note taped on top.

"Thought you might need these. Take care of yourself until I get back. Cash."

"Don't you even think about crying," she warned herself as she cut a brownie, took a bite, then put it down to open the fridge to get the milk.

The note made her feel better. That and the brownie. As she pulled the milk carton from the fridge, she heard the sound of a footfall.

Only this time it wasn't upstairs. This time, it was right behind her.

She spun around with the milk carton in her hand, two thoughts crowding together. *Run! Scream!*

But she didn't get the chance to do either. The milk carton hit the kitchen floor, burst. Milk pooled on the floor like fresh blood as she stared at the barrel of the gun pointed at her heart.

"Don't make a sound or I'll kill you."

THE ROAD OUT TO the old Trayton place seemed farther than usual. Cash couldn't think about anything but Molly. He hated leaving her. Even with three armed guards. It was all he could do not to tell Mathews to turn the car around and take him back. He had a bad feeling, one he couldn't shake.

"You all right?" Mathews said with a sideways glance.

"Just worried about Molly," he said.

"She's in good hands. Anyway, I have a feeling that is one woman who can take care of herself."

Cash fell silent. He didn't doubt Mathews's words. But the past few days he'd fallen into the habit of taking care of her. It was a habit he didn't want to break.

He remembered that he hadn't heard back from Frank. Molly could be wanted for just about anything. She could be facing criminal charges and a long prison term. He closed his eyes to the thought.

He felt Mathews turn off on the back road, one that the killer shouldn't know about. The old barn wasn't far off the main highway, easily seen by anyone looking for a place to hide a car. Or a body.

The patrol car slowed, then stopped. Mathews turned off the engine and the lights. They sat for moment in the darkness, then Cash heard him pop the trunk. He opened his door and got out, Mathews doing the same.

They were on the far side of the farm, hidden by a small hill. From here they would walk.

Cash followed him around to the trunk. Mathews reached in and took out two shotguns. He handed one to Cash along with a look. He was touched by Mathews trust in him—but if things went badly tonight, heads would roll.

After tonight, he would tell Mathews everything. He just hoped he wouldn't lose his job over it. But with luck, Jasmine's killer would be behind bars after tonight. Her body recovered and laid to rest. His name cleared. And Molly? He just prayed that she would be safe until he returned. And she would be as long as Vince and Angel didn't realize they'd been duped and doubled back.

With any luck, a highway patrolman already had the two men in custody.

Cash took the shotgun Mathews handed him. He also had his service revolver.

"Ready?" Mathews asked.

He nodded and Mathews softly closed the trunk.

They walked up over the hill through the dark night. Clouds scudded overhead covering the moon. A few stars glittered through the clouds. They moved quickly, taking advantage of the lack of moonlight.

Below them, the lake's surface was hammered pewter. Cash could smell the water. A restless breeze rustled the cottonwoods as they moved along the north shore.

Ahead, he could make out a dark smudge on the horizon, beyond it, the broken, jagged roof of the old barn where Jasmine's car had been found.

Cash heard the sound of the vehicle at the same instant Mathews did. They both stopped to listen, their gazes meeting in the darkness. Someone was coming up the road toward the old farm. Someone driving with his headlights off.

Cash moved quickly toward the stand of pines from

where they would have a good view of the barn and the rest of the farm. Overhead, the clouds parted. A shaft of moonlight beamed down as they ducked into the darkness of the pines, disappearing from view.

The sound of the engine rumbled as the vehicle drove along the bumpy road. Every once in a while, Cash would catch the flicker of brake lights as the driver slowly moved on the rutted road.

Mathews looked over at him as he heard the vehicle stop, the sound of the engine dying into silence. The night settled around them. Cash could see the dark shape of the car but couldn't tell the make.

He realized he was holding his breath. A car door opened and then closed quietly. Someone stepped away from the vehicle, just a shadow of a figure moving through the darkness, headed directly toward them. A man. He was carrying a shovel.

Chapter Fifteen

Molly didn't feel the milk carton slip from her fingers, didn't hear it hit the floor and burst open, didn't notice the spray soak the hem of her jeans.

She stared at the gun in Patty Franklin's hand, her mind telling her *This isn't happening.*

Jasmine's former roommate smiled. "Surprised to see me, Jasmine?"

"Patty, I'm not—"

"Don't even bother. You might be able to fool the others but remember me? What did I hear you tell Bernard one time, that I was 'dumb as dirt and just as interesting'? But there is an advantage to being invisible. No one notices me so I hear and see things, Jasmine."

Molly's mind raced. It didn't make any sense. Molly had been so sure that the killer would go to the farm, check Jasmine's grave, not chance another murder until he was sure. Cash would never have left her if he thought there was any chance the killer would come here.

Because Patty wasn't the killer. She'd just come here, angry at Jasmine. But how had she gotten past the three men guarding the house?

Patty smiled as if reading her mind. "I was in the house all the time. Your boyfriend didn't even see me. Another benefit of being small and mousy. I practically blend into the wallpaper."

So she hadn't even heard about the search being called off at the farm. Had she heard about the plan? "Cash and the state investigator will be back soon."

Patty smiled. "I don't think so. I would imagine they're out at the farm waiting for Jasmine's killer to show them where she's buried."

So she had heard the plan. She knew Cash and Mathews wouldn't be back, probably for a long time. "But there are three men outside," Molly said.

"And if you try to alert them I will kill you before you and I have our talk," Patty said. "And in case you really do have amnesia and don't remember, I'm an exceptional shot with a gun. I'm just not as good with a rock."

A rock? Shock rippled through her. Molly's blood ran cold at the thought of Jasmine's head injury. "*You* killed Jasmine?"

"I'm starting to believe that you don't remember what we said to each other that night in the Dew Drop Inn parking lot before I killed you the first time," Patty said.

Distracting Patty would be next to impossible. The woman seemed unshakable. Time might be the only chance Molly had. Maybe Cash and Mathews could come back for some reason. "I told you I don't remember because—"

"Because you aren't Jasmine. You even fooled the sheriff and the state investigator. I saw you with your suitcase earlier. You just got rid of them so you could take off again."

Molly groaned. Nothing she could say to Patty would convince her she wasn't Jasmine. She saw it clearly now, the reason Patty hadn't gone out to the grave. Patty wanted her to be Jasmine, wanted her to be alive—so she could kill her again.

That's why she wasn't worried about the three men outside. The moment Patty pulled the trigger they would come busting in here. She couldn't possibly get away with this. But she didn't care.

Patty's expression was that of a woman about to commit murder. There was little emotion in the single-minded way Patty held the gun. No wavering. She didn't even seem nervous. What she seemed was determined. Patty had come here to kill her. Plain and simple.

"It's over," Patty said. "But at least this time I will make sure I take you with me. This time you're going to *stay* dead."

"Jasmine *is* dead, Patty. You're making a terrible mistake. You killed her the first time. If you kill me it will be for nothing. Jasmine's wherever you buried her."

"I didn't bury you," Patty said. "I just left you behind the steering wheel of your car. I checked your pulse. I was so sure you were dead."

Molly stared at her. "Then how did the car end up in a barn outside of Antelope Flats?"

"I have no idea. Why don't you tell me? Didn't you put it there to frame the sheriff?"

Molly's head was spinning. None of this made any sense.

"I wish I'd pushed your car off a cliff instead of just leaving it in front of the bar," Patty said. "It would have made things so much easier."

"What bar?"

"The Dew Drop Inn, of course." Patty cocked her head. "Don't tell me you can't remember what we fought about."

"In case you really care, my name is Molly Kilpatrick." Molly tried to remember what was on the kitchen counter behind her. "My father was killed after a diamond heist in Hollywood." Back when she worked with her father she could have recalled everything that was there in the proper placement. But she was out of practice. "I'm pretending to be Jasmine because there are two killers after me."

"I heard that story when I was listening on the stairs," Patty said.

"It's true." Molly inched back toward the kitchen counter, praying there was something she could use to defend herself. But she couldn't imagine what, especially against a gun. "My father hid the diamonds and now his partners just got out of prison and think I know where the diamonds are. They plan to kill me."

"They aren't going to get the chance if you move again," Patty said, no emotion in her voice. "Even if these two killers existed, I will shoot you first."

Molly froze, seeing she meant it. "So tell me what

it was you and Jasmine fought about the night you killed her."

Patty smiled. "I have some things to say to you, Jasmine. Last time you did all the talking until I shut you up with that rock. This time, I'll do the talking." Patty glared at her. "Since you don't remember...I was waiting for you when you came out of the bar. You'd just had a big fight with someone. Either your brother or Kerrington since I knew you'd been with them. Whoever it was had shoved you. You'd hit your head. It was bleeding. You were in one of your foul moods. I noticed when I was waiting that one of the headlights on that new car you were so proud of was out and when I got closer, I saw that the right front fender was smashed. I asked you what had happened, but you said you didn't have time for my 'mindless prattle.'"

Patty took a breath, shifted from one foot to the other, her eyes a little glazed as if lost in the past. But Molly knew that before she could move, Patty could get off several shots at this close range.

"You were furious because the sheriff had crashed his pickup into your brand new expensive car," Patty continued. "I *loved* it. Finally someone had stood up to you. He'd caught you with Kerrington. All your games with him were over. He threatened to go to your father if you didn't take back that announcement you'd made about being engaged to him. You were beside yourself. No one walked away from you. You'd get him back. You'd show him. Then you'd break him. And Kerrington, too. You'd found out that Kerrington wasn't just dating Sandra but that he'd gotten her pregnant and was going to have to marry her. You were going to destroy both of them, too."

Molly felt sick. Had Jasmine really been that vicious? "Jasmine must have been nice some time. Otherwise, why did any of you put up with her?" For a moment Molly didn't think she was going to answer her.

"You were nice at first. You did these little thoughtful things like buy us a pair of earrings or bring us a latte. You seemed to care." Her voice took on a bitter edge. "You got us to tell you our deepest, darkest secrets, things we'd never told anyone, and later, when you turned on us and used those secrets against us, *you* always managed to come off as the victim, the one who was so hurt that we would think you would ever do anything like that."

Molly felt a cold chill skitter up her spine. What horrible thing had she done to this woman to push her to this point? "What did I do to you?"

"I loved him." Patty's voice broke. It was the first emotion Molly had seen and she knew she'd hit a nerve.

"Kerrington?"

Patty's headed snapped back in surprise. "No. Bernard."

"Bernard?" Molly couldn't have been more shocked.

Patty was looking at her strangely. "You *really* don't remember." She gripped the gun a little tighter. "You said you would talk to him about me." Her eyes shone brightly in the kitchen light. "You said you would tell him the good things about me."

Molly could see what was coming.

Patty's eyes brimmed with tears. "When he asked

me out, I was so excited. You did my hair and make-up. You said I looked beautiful. You said he wouldn't be able to resist me, once he saw me, once he got to know me."

Molly felt her own tears. She didn't want to hear anymore. "I'm so sorry, Patty."

But Patty wasn't listening. She was reliving the humiliation of that night, a humiliation Molly didn't even want to imagine.

A sob escaped Patty's lips. She choked back another. "It was all a joke. On me. A big laugh for you."

Molly saw her fingers tighten again on the gun and knew she didn't have much time now. Could one of the men outside get in fast enough to save her if she screamed and dove for the door?

Something moved behind Patty. A stealth shadow. Cash had come back? Or maybe one of the guards had come in to check on her?

Except the doors were all locked. So were the windows. Whoever had come in either had a key. Or…Molly felt her pulse jump. Or had broken into the house.

The shadow moved closer just behind Patty, drawing Molly's attention. Patty saw Molly's eyes dart to a spot over her shoulder. She swung, trying to bring the gun around, but before she could fire a shot, Angel was on her, wrenching the gun from her hand.

Patty cried out and dropped to her knees. Angel stuck the weapon into the waist of his pants and put a knife to Patty's throat, but his eyes were on Molly as if daring her to move.

"Looks like it was a good thing we came back when we did, Vince," Angel said.

FROM THE STAND OF PINES, Cash froze as he watched the figure move through the darkness toward them, carrying the shovel.

Cash could sense Mathews next to him, thinking no doubt the same thing he was. What if the body was buried in the pines where they stood?

They didn't dare move, didn't hardly breathe for fear whoever was coming toward them would see or hear them and take off.

The man appeared as a silhouette against the horizon. He walked awkwardly across the uneven ground in the pitch blackness of the cloudy night, the shovel in his right hand.

Just when Cash knew they would be discovered if the man came any closer, he stopped just inside the pine grove, picked up a large rock and threw it aside. Cash heard the sound of metal scrape dirt as the man began to dig.

Cash silently let out the breath he'd been holding, his relief almost as great as his grief. Finally, Jasmine would be found. Whatever Jasmine had done in her life, she deserved to be put to rest. Cash leaned back against the tree to wait.

The digging stopped. The man threw down the shovel and knelt on the ground.

Beside Cash, Mathews motioned it was time. They moved in quickly, weapons drawn.

If the grave digger heard them coming, he didn't

have time to react. Cash sprung from the trees, covering the short distance in a matter of a few strides, the shotgun in his hands.

The man was kneeling on one knee next to the grave. Cash pressed the end of the shotgun barrel against the man's right ear. "Freeze! Police!"

Mathews flicked on his flashlight and shone it into the man's face, then into the partially opened grave, the light ricocheting off a skull.

Kerrington blinked, blinded by the light. He let out a sound like a sob and dropped to his other knee. "It isn't what you think," he cried. "I didn't kill her. I swear to God, she didn't fall hard enough to kill her."

Sick to his stomach, Cash pressed the barrel into Kerrington's neck.

"I'll get the patrol car," Mathews said, looking up at Cash, a clear warning in his gaze. "Read him his rights."

"You have the right to remain silent," Cash began.

"You have to believe me. I shoved her. Outside the bar and she fell and hit her head, but she was alive. She was furious because you'd ran into her new car and…because Sandra had told her that she was pregnant and we were getting married. I told her I wouldn't marry Sandra, but she was so angry. She was hitting me. I pushed her, she fell. I saw that her head was bleeding and I tried to get her to let me look at it but she wouldn't." His voice broke. "I went back into the bar but I was worried about her. She was in such a state. I went back outside. She was sitting in her car, leaning over the steering wheel. I thought she was just upset, maybe crying." Kerrington began to sob. "There was blood all over." He wrapped his arms around his knees, put his head on the ground next to her grave. "I loved her. I would never kill her."

Cash finished reading him his rights. He could hear Mathews coming with the patrol car. "If you didn't kill her, how did you know where she was buried?"

Kerrington wiped a sleeve over his face and raised his head. "I had to do something. I panicked. I shoved her over in the seat and climbed in. When I looked up, I saw the bartender. She'd come outside for a quick smoke. I didn't know how much she'd seen. I hoped she thought Jasmine was just drunk and that I was driving her home. But I knew she'd seen us fighting before that. Maybe even seen me shove her."

"Why did you put her car in this barn?" Cash asked, already knowing the answer.

"She'd had that fight with you. You'd dented her car. I thought…" His voice trailed off. "I wasn't really trying to frame you. After what I did, I couldn't call the cops and tell them where I'd put it. I guess I hoped the car wouldn't ever be found."

"You didn't want to implicate yourself," Cash said. "You were worried that there would be evidence in the car that might incriminate you."

Mathews pulled up, the headlights of the patrol car bobbing across Jasmine's grave.

"Let's go," Cash said and helped Kerrington to his feet before cuffing him and escorting him into the back of the patrol car.

"I called forensics to see about the body," Mathews said and looked over at him as Cash climbed into the front seat. "I've been trying to reach one of my men at your house."

Cash's blood turned to ice. Molly. No.

"No one's answering." Mathews hit the siren and lights as he sped toward town.

MOLLY STEPPED BACK, the counter cutting into her back as Angel slapped Patty, flattening her on the floor. In that instant, Molly had a flash of memory. There was a cof-feemaker on the counter, a bear-sheriff cookie jar, ob-viously a present, probably from Cash's little sister Dusty. An old blender. And the small vase Cash had put her wildflowers in that morning when he'd brought her breakfast in bed.

"Molly," Angel said and grinned. "It is so good to fi-nally see you." There was just enough sarcasm in his greeting to warn her as he swung with his free hand.

He would have hit Molly if she hadn't seen it com-ing and ducked.

She swung down and around, grabbing the heavy glass of the blender as she came up. She swung it like a club. The blender struck Angel's right hand—the hand with the knife in it—as he dove for her.

He let out a howl. The knife went flying, hit the floor and slid under the stove.

"You bitch," Angel yelled and lunged for her again.

Molly tried to get in position to swing the blender again, but Angel had moved too quickly. She ducked, flinching in expectation of the pain that would no doubt come from Angel's fury.

"Angel, wait!"

Vince stepped between them. "It's all right, Molly." His voice was soft, reassuring.

She wasn't fooled. She remembered both men only too well and knew exactly what they were capable of from listening in on their conversations when she was fourteen.

She stood slowly, still gripping the heavy glass blender. Patty was on the floor in the kitchen doorway slumped like a rag doll but conscious. Molly could see that her eyes were open and she was still breathing.

"You can put that down now," Vince said in that same quiet deep voice. "No one wants to hurt you."

Molly laughed, a half-hysterical sound. Everyone in this room wanted to kill her. At least Patty would have made it quick.

Vince smiled as if seeing the humor as well.

"You said I could have the bitch," Angel said. He was hunched against the far end of the counter holding his injured right hand. "I think she broke my friggin' fingers."

She could only hope that he wasn't as expert with a knife in his left hand as he was his right.

"Let's all just calm down," Vince said. "Molly, Molly, Molly." He sighed. "Why would you put the cops on us? You know what we want. Just give it to us and we'll be on our way."

He was lying and she suspected everyone in this room knew it, even Patty who'd never laid eyes on either man before.

"I don't have the diamonds, Vince," Molly said, knowing he wasn't going to believe her anymore than Patty had believed she wasn't Jasmine.

"I told you the bitch would just lie," Angel snapped.

Vince motioned for Angel to be quiet. "I saw Max whisper something to you, Molly."

She nodded, adjusting her hold on the blender. Vince didn't have a weapon. At least not in his hands. Angel had Patty's pistol still tucked into the waistband of his pants, but he seemed to have forgotten about it in his pain. He kept rubbing his right hand, glaring at her.

"All Max said was 'I'm sorry, kiddo. I'll try to make it up to you.'"

Vince stared at her in disbelief. "Are you telling me Max would waste his last words on something so…ridiculous? How could he possibly make it up to you? He had to know he was dying."

"He said that to me every time one of his schemes failed," Molly said, unable to hide her own bitterness. Max was her only family and he was dead because he was always trying to find the easy way out.

"You knew him," Molly said, finding herself getting angry. "You think he ever made my life easy, even once? Max took the diamonds, to hell with him. It's obviously the way he wanted it."

"She's lying," Angel said. "Let me get the truth out of her."

Vince just looked at her, then sighed, and she noticed then how much he'd aged. He looked as strong as a bull but his face was gray, his eyes lifeless.

He looked over at Angel and she saw that Vince had given up. He might believe her, but it didn't make any difference at this point.

"She's all yours," he said to Angel and turned, stepping over Patty as he left the room.

"Vince," Molly called, but knew he wasn't going to save her. She heard the creak of the door that opened the bar, heard him pour himself a drink and sit down as if the weight of the world were on him.

It didn't matter if she knew where the diamonds were or not. Vince wouldn't—or couldn't—stop Angel now.

Angel grinned, spittle at the corner of his mouth as if salivating at the thought of torturing her to death.

He took Patty's small pistol from the waist of his pants and tossed it on the kitchen counter with contempt. Then he edged slowly toward her, opening one kitchen drawer after another until he found what he was after.

He drew a large butcher knife from the drawer with his left hand, his grin spreading across his face, making him look crazy. "Lucky for me I'm ambidextrous."

He lunged at her. She swung the blender, but he was ready, catching it with his right forearm. The heavy glass ricocheted off his arm, hit the edge of the counter and shattered, showering them both with glass as Angel grabbed a handful of her hair with his injured right hand and brought his knee up, catching her in the thigh.

She cried out and he dropped her to the floor, her leg cramping in pain, and he was on her, the butcher knife at her neck, his voice in her ear.

"Now, first off I want you to apologize for putting the cops on us," he whispered. "Then I want you to tell me where the diamonds are. And finally, I want to hear you beg for your life. And you will beg, trust me."

MATHEWS HAD THE PATROL CAR up to over a hundred as they raced toward town, the siren blaring, lights flashing.

With growing fear, Cash tried to reach the officers Mathews had left at the house and got no answer on the two-way radio.

Cash looked over at Mathews as they neared town. Mathews cut the lights and siren, stopping up the street from the house. Cash leapt from the car before it completely stopped, the shotgun in his hands as he ran in a crouch toward the house.

The lights were on inside. No cars out front. No one outside either. Nor did the officers appear as he ran toward the front door. Mathews motioned he was going around the back. Molly would have locked the door, but he tried it anyway before he pulled out his key and quietly put it into the lock.

From inside the house, Cash heard a scream.

His fingers shaking, he turned the knob and burst into the house, the shotgun ready.

The first thing he saw was Patty Franklin curled on the floor in the kitchen doorway. At first he didn't recognize her. Her mascara had run and there was a bright red mark on the side of her face as if she'd recently been slapped.

But her face came alive when she saw him.

His forward motion propelled Cash on into the house. Out of the corner of his eye, he saw a large man sitting in the living room. Vince Winslow shot to his feet. He lunged at Cash, but Patty caught his leg, tripping him and biting down hard on his calf. Vince let out a curse and turned to kick Patty.

Cash brought the butt of the shotgun down on Vince's head. He hit the floor hard, out like a light.

Patty motioned to the kitchen and put a finger across her throat like a knife. Cash went cold. He nodded and stepped into the kitchen.

What he saw almost made him lose control. The short one, Angel Edwards, had Molly on her hands and knees on the floor, a knife to her throat as he leaned over her. There was blood already running down her neck from several cuts. Her eyes were wide. She blinked at him, her expression softening at the sight of him. There was broken glass all around her on the floor. And blood.

"Get off her," Cash said between gritted teeth.

"I'll slit her throat before you can pull that trigger," Angel said, glee in his voice. "You might kill me, but you'll never be able to save her."

Angel hadn't noticed Patty come into the kitchen. Cash had hardly noticed her himself. She moved almost in slow motion, her hands behind her, no expression on her face.

"Now, put down that shotgun," Angel was saying. "Or I'll kill her. Now!" he shrieked, jerking back on Molly's hair.

It happened so fast Cash wasn't even sure he saw it. Molly let out a cry as Angel jerked her head back. Her hands had been on the floor, but now she came up with a large piece of the broken glass. She drove the glass into Angel's calf as she screamed, "Shoot him!"

Didn't she realize he couldn't fire the shotgun—not with her so close?

But the room boomed with a gunshot, then another,

and Cash watched in amazement as Patty rushed Angel, firing a small pistol point blank at his head. Where had she gotten that?

Angel had let go of Molly when she gouged him with the broken glass, but he still had the knife in one hand and a fistful of her hair in the other.

That was until he saw Patty running at him, firing the gun he had so carelessly tossed aside. The caliber was too small to put a man like Angel down.

Patty had been shooting over both Angel's and Molly's heads, but when he saw her running at him firing the gun, he let go of Molly's hair and lunged for Patty.

Molly rolled, flattening herself on the kitchen floor. Cash pulled the trigger, the shotgun bucked in his hands. Angel's chest bloomed with blood just an instant before he swung the blade of the butcher knife in his hand toward Patty.

Cash reached for her to pull her back but it was too late. Angel drove the knife into her chest, letting go as he fell to the floor.

Patty stumbled, falling to her knees. Molly was on her feet, rushing to her, catching her and lowering her to the floor as Cash saw Angel reach for the pistol Patty had dropped.

Cash stepped down hard on Angel's hand. He was still alive, staring up at Cash, bloodthirsty to the end.

"I'm not going back to prison," Angel said.

"You're right about that," Cash said and watched Angel die.

Behind him, he heard Mathews come into the room.

He was on his two-way radioing for an ambulance and backup.

Cash knelt on the floor next to Molly. She had Patty's head in her lap and she was crying.

"I'm so sorry," Molly was whispering. "I'm so sorry."

Patty's eyes flickered open. She smiled up at Molly. "You're not Jasmine."

Molly shook her head.

"It's all right. I'll be seeing her soon." Patty's eyes glittered at the thought for a moment, then the light went out and slowly her lids closed and she was gone.

Molly leaned over, crying. Cash put an arm around her, drawing her to him as Mathews took the dead woman from her.

"It's over, Molly. It's finally all over. You're safe." Cash held her to him, wishing he never had to let her go.

Epilogue

Cash watched Molly peer out the plane window and smiled to himself to see how well she was recovering.

"I can't believe this is the first time I've ever flown," she said, her excitement contagious. "Thank you for coming with me."

Past her profile, the Atlantic Ocean shone deep blue as the plane made the final approach to the Miami International Airport.

He'd been in the E.R. waiting room, waiting to hear how Molly was doing from the cuts on her neck, when he'd gotten the call from Frank. Mathews had arrested Vince when he came to and had the coroner pick up Patty and Angel. Vince was back in prison and wouldn't be getting out any time soon.

Kerrington had been arrested for his part in covering up Jasmine's death—and the murder of Teresa Clark. Kerrington swore he hadn't killed the bartender, that Bernard must have done it. Kerrington was in jail in Montana, on no bond, awaiting trial. His wife Sandra had filed for divorce and had moved in with Bernard.

Bernard had confessed, now that Jasmine's killer had been caught. He had admitted that he had been the man the gas station clerk had seen leave with Jasmine. He hadn't come forward because of obvious reasons. He'd said he and Jasmine had talked and then she'd gone to meet Kerrington. He'd said that was the last time he'd seen her and that the bartender had been wrong about him being at the Dew Drop Inn the night Jasmine had been killed.

Bernard had seen that Jasmine was properly buried in Atlanta next to her father.

Mathews was still investigating Teresa Clark's murder, convinced that before it was over, Bernard would be behind bars where he belonged.

Cash had asked for a few weeks off after receiving Frank's call from the FBI.

"Cash, sorry man, I know it's late, but I thought you'd want this news ASAP."

Cash had completely forgotten that Molly's prints were on file somewhere and he'd asked Frank to track them down. It seemed like a lifetime ago—not just hours.

He had started to tell Frank that it didn't matter. He didn't care what she'd done. Or who she was. "Frank, right now isn't—"

"You aren't going to believe this. I tracked down those prints you sent me. Her name's Molly right? It was a kidnapping."

"She's wanted for *kidnapping?*"

"Naw." Frank had laughed. "She *was* kidnapped. Almost thirty years ago. Biological father stole her. Mother never saw her again, later the mother had reason to believe she was dead after the private investigators she'd hired almost caught the father. Found some of the toddler's clothing with a whole lot of blood on it where the two had been staying. Turned out to be the toddler's blood type."

Was that when Molly had gotten the scar on her forehead that she couldn't remember getting? "Is her mother still alive?" Cash had asked.

"Affirmative. That's what makes this case so interesting. This isn't just any kid who was kidnapped. This is the daughter of Rachel Valentine of the Paris Valentines, one of the wealthiest families in Europe."

There had to be a mistake. Molly was a Valentine?

"It gets better. Guess who the father was."

"The Great Maximilian Burke."

"You knew, huh? Well, then you must know about the big diamond heist in Hollywood fifteen years ago. He was shot down by the cops. The diamonds were never recovered. When they took his prints they found out that he was Joe Cooper, the man the FBI had been looking for in the kidnapping of the Valentine baby. But the Valentines paid to keep all that quiet, hoping to find the kid. She would have been fourteen then."

Cash had a feeling he knew what was coming.

"Someone had seen a girl about the right age with Maximilian right before he died, but she disappeared. No one knew what had happened to her. Might not even have been his daughter. According to the guys who were arrested, she *wasn't* his daughter, just some girl he'd picked up to help him with his magic acts," Frank had said. "Whoever she was, she'd just disappeared.

"The thing is," Frank had continued, "the agents really want to talk to this woman. The diamonds in that heist were never found and since she was the last person to see Maximilian alive... Tell me you have her in custody."

"Sorry. Maybe she'll turn up again," Cash had said, afraid he really was going to lose her. "Where'd you say her mother lives?"

"Miami. I can't believe you let her get away," Frank had said and Cash had looked up and seen the doctor coming down the hall toward him.

"Got to go. Thanks, Frank." He'd hung up.

"She's going to be fine," the doctor had said. "Fortunately the cuts were superficial. She might have a couple of light scars, nothing like the one on her forehead. She tell you how she got that one?"

Cash had shaken his head. "She doesn't remember."

"Nasty scar. Must have really bled. I've given her some pain medicine and prescribed some more if she needs it." He'd handed Cash the prescription. "She said she was with you?"

Cash had nodded. "She's with me."

"I'm scared," Molly said now as the plane made its descent into Miami.

He took her hand and squeezed it gently. She squeezed back. He knew it wasn't the landing that had her frightened. It was meeting her mother. Molly had had no idea her mother was still alive. Or that her father had kidnapped her.

"It explains why we never stayed in one place for long," she'd said when he'd told her the news. "Also why he didn't want anyone to know he was my father."

Rachel Valentine had been overjoyed to hear that her daughter had finally been found. And she'd put together the last piece of the puzzle.

"Max sent me Molly's teddy bear," Rachel said, tears in her voice. "I got it in the mail fifteen years ago with a note. All the note said was that he was sorry and that he would someday make it up to me."

The FBI agent Cash sent to check the teddy bear found the stolen diamonds from the heist inside.

The plane touched down. Cash could feel how anxious Molly was—and how worried. Molly and her mother would be strangers. Mothers shouldn't be strangers to their children, he thought, thinking of his own mother.

Except Rachel Valentine hadn't chosen this. She'd spent years and thousands of dollars trying to find Molly. She'd only given up when she'd thought Molly was dead. Later, when Max had been killed, she'd tried again but to no avail. Molly had been running again.

Cash was just thankful that she'd run to him.

The limo that Rachel Valentine had sent for her daughter was waiting as they came out of the terminal. When the chauffeur jumped out and opened the door, a beautiful woman with blond hair and green eyes disembarked from the back. The resemblance between the two women left little doubt that Molly was her long-lost daughter.

Rachel froze at the sight of Molly, her hand going to her mouth, tears brimming in her eyes. Then she opened her arms and Molly stumbled into them.

Cash watched the two hug. They had almost thirty

years of catching up to do. He'd promised to come this far with Molly, but now she would be fine on her own. Molly was a strong woman. She'd already survived so much.

He turned to disappear into the crowd. Molly didn't need him anymore.

"Cash?"

He stopped at the sound of her voice, amazed by the effect it always had on him. He turned slowly to look at her. She couldn't have been more beautiful standing there beside her mother.

She smiled at him as she walked to him. "Where do you think you're going?"

"Molly, you don't need me now. You and your mother have a lot of catching up to do. You're finally safe, with family. Who knows, you might decide to stay in Miami." He looked to the palm trees waving in the sea breeze. "It's beautiful here."

She touched his cheek, drawing his gaze back to hers. "This is just a visit. One of many I hope. For the first time in my life, I've found the place I want to stay, Cash. It's a little town in Montana. Antelope Flats. Ever heard of it?"

"Molly, you don't know what you're saying."

"I spent my whole life running from something I never understood." She touched the scar on her forehead, a head wound from a childhood accident that had bled enough to make her mother stop looking for her.

"I don't want to run anymore, especially from my feelings," she said. "I'm in love with you, Cash McCall. We don't know each other very well, but I was thinking that if I were to hang around Antelope Flats, maybe we could get to know each other."

His heart swelled and for a moment he couldn't say a word. He looked into her eyes, reminded of a spring day in Montana, and thought he caught a glimpse of the future. He pulled her into his arms, closing his eyes and just holding her.

"About that old house of yours," she said when she finally drew back.

"I'll put it on the market when I get back to Montana," he said.

"You bought it because you like old houses, right?"

He nodded, looking embarrassed. "You hate old houses."

She smiled. "I used to, but I have to tell you I've been thinking about your house. It would take a lot of work, but it has...possibilities. Just like you and me."

"Are you sure?" Cash asked, his heart in his throat. "That house has to have some bad memories for you."

She shook her head. "I've run my whole life from bad memories. That house also has some good memories and I'm hoping to make a lot more once I get back to Montana." She smiled. "Which will be soon." She kissed him then, a soft, sweet kiss filled with promise, then she turned and walked back to her mother and disappeared into the back of the limo.

Cash watched her go, turned and, whistling, headed for home. Home. The day he'd bought it, he'd dreamed of someday finding a woman to love and filling that old house with children.

What he'd never dreamed of was a woman like Molly. Some things were even beyond a man's wildest dreams.

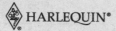

SPOTLIGHT

National bestselling author

JOANNA WAYNE

The Gentlemen's Club

A homicide in the French Quarter of New Orleans has attorney Rachel Powers obsessed with finding the killer. As she investigates, she is shocked to discover that some of the Big Easy's most respected gentlemen will go to any lengths to satisfy their darkest sexual desires. Even murder.

*A gripping new novel...
coming in June.*

HARLEQUIN®
Live the emotion™

**Bonus Features,
including:**

**Author Interview,
Romance—
New Orleans Style,
and Bonus Read!**

eHARLEQUIN.com

The Ultimate Destination for Women's Fiction

For **FREE online reading,** visit
www.eHarlequin.com now and enjoy:

Online Reads
Read **Daily** and **Weekly** chapters from
our Internet-exclusive stories by your
favorite authors.

Interactive Novels
Cast your vote to help decide how these
stories unfold...then stay tuned!

Quick Reads
For shorter romantic reads, try our
collection of Poems, Toasts, & More!

Online Read Library
Miss one of our online reads?
Come here to catch up!

Reading Groups
Discuss, share and rave with other
community members!

For great reading online,
visit www.eHarlequin.com today!

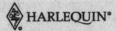